Hatching Day... is not too great.

Darkness.

Well...

Not quite darkness. A dim, warm light surrounds him, but it's muted, as if traveling through a barrier of sorts. He breathes, but he's curled so tightly that it's hard to draw in a good breath. Walls surround him on all sides, enclosing him into a tiny, curled position. He can feel his heart rate rise as panic sets in and he takes another too-small, too-shallow breath.

He starts scrabbling at the walls around him. Strange scraping noises accompany him, as if he has claws instead of hands.

Where am I? Wasn't I just heading to class?

I had picked up my bookbag and was heading to school. Mrs. Lassiter was outside watering her flowers just like every morning, even though she only has a small box of them outside her apartment. I could smell the Jiangs cooking their usual breakfast from down the hall and hurried past before Song could try to flirt with me...

Reborn as a Defective Drake: Snoweldon's Dragon

Where has all the air gone? He wiggles as much as possible, but it feels as if there's nothing left in this hot, wet place to breathe in!

Again, he claws frantically at the walls; and finally, one of his fingers catches and breaks through to sweet, sweet air!

He uses both hands now, frantically pulling at the round enclosure that confines him. It comes off in strange, fragile pieces colored a pale, silver-speckled cream. Finally, he opens the space of about two hands in the wall and just sits a moment, breathing in the fresh air that and bright beams of light that enter into his strange entrapment. Breathing is good, he thinks groggily. Somehow, he is exhausted from all that has happened. So instead, he props his head next to the crack so that his pale, oddly long nose can poke through and just sits there, too fatigued to move much further.

The elevator ride down had been fine, a little noisy, and it had frozen up once, but I had still made it down safely. The sharp scent of gasoline and exhaust had met me in the car park, but that was fine too. I had hurriedly hopped onto my moped and sped out of there, heading north towards my university. Only a few more moments, and I should have arrived at school in time for my eight-o'clock linear algebra class.

I had stopped at an intersection, waiting for my light. Near my side of the road, I saw a construction site. It had been interesting, and I had been calculating how many

Reborn as a Defective Drake: Snoweldon's Dragon

Book illustrations by Savanah Townley

Editing by Laura Grace Terry and Trudy Shadrick

www.isekaidragon.com

Table Of Contents

Reborn as a Defective Drake: Snoweldon's Dragon

tons of metal were being lifted by the crane and what kind of cables had to be used to withstand it. But then, I heard an odd sound.

It was kind of like a dead donkey, or rather, what I imagined a dead donkey would sound like if someone brought it back to life and whipped it until it brayed. From behind me, I heard the tell-tale sound of ugly rap music and northern slang.

"Whatchoo doin' here, tighty-whitey?" Jackson Rittz called from his banged up Jeep. I pretended I didn't notice and fervently hoped for the light to change soon. Why did he have to be a jerk? Really, he should get a life!

"Oi, Goody-two-shoes! We missed you at the party last night! You coulda been lit!" Jeff Winston catcalled from Jackson's left.

"Yeah, as the freaking trash can!" Lucy Lopez cackled from the back where she was sitting on her boyfriend's lap. "Get it, because you're white trash that even the government won't support."

I felt my irritation peak. Really? Just because I had to work instead of relying on government aid for my schooling?

"Yeah. Real mature, guys. Real mature." I grumbled softly and quickly gunned the engine as the light turned green. Good thing they still didn't know where I lived. I'd hate to see what kind of crap they could pull...

Reborn as a Defective Drake: Snoweldon's Dragon

The route to university wasn't inordinately long, but today I felt as if it was, if only because noisy catcalls and stupid taunts kept popping up at every light. Finally, I spotted a yellow light and gunned my moped, trying to get across the intersection and leave them stranded. The light turned red just as I entered the intersection and a huge shadow fell over me with the loud sound of a car horn...

Instead of moving, he looks around at his strangely rounded prison while he waits for his body to recover. For a prison or cage, it's weird. White goop coats the walls and himself, and an oddly creamy membrane covers the walls. Red veins trace through the rounded enclosure, kind of like blood vessels or something, and he has a few moments of horror as he wonders if he's been eaten in the first alien invasion. Only, the white stuff doesn't sting like he would think stomach acid would, and stomach linings are normally composed of muscle to facilitate digesting things anyway. He looks down at the oddly rounded bottom of the prison where most of the white goop has pooled. Most of his body is hidden under the white stuff, but he still sees oddly white, skinny arms curled up against a similarly colored chest. Yet, what gets his attention is the fact that his hands are not exactly hands. They are...scaly with four digits...and somewhat cutely clawed tips. There are even dew claws on what he supposes, somewhat hysterically, are actually his forelegs rather than his arms.

What has happened to him? He can't stop staring at his

Reborn as a Defective Drake: Snoweldon's Dragon

hands. They're obviously not human. Instead, his hands look like a strange mix of bird and big cat. He has four long, forward-facing... toes? These are tipped with short colorless claws, and he somehow knows that if he flexes his...paws a certain way, those short, cute little nails will lengthen into something not nearly as short or cute. Shifting his neck reveals another inhuman factor to his body; he now has an inordinately long neck. Though, it isn't as long as a giraffe's neck, so he supposes that it could be worse. Shifting it even slightly changes his point of view drastically.

Now that he thinks about it, he didn't used to be able to see his nose like that either. It's long, like a snout, and a bright white just like the rest of him. He opens his jaw and wishes that he had a reflective surface to look into. Does he have pointy teeth? He licks his teeth, and while he manages to avoid slicing his tongue open, he does come to a very important conclusion. Yes, he now has sharp teeth, and his tongue is most definitely as long as a Looney Tunes character's tongue.

Pain, believe it or not, was actually not the first thing I noticed. The first thing I noticed was flying through the air. My moped went in one direction, and I went in the other. I had a front row seat to seeing my precious Yamaha go straight through the little hotdog stand on the corner. It then proceeded to tumble through the window of the Starbucks behind it, though I only just barely noticed that as gravity reintroduced my body to the ground.

Reborn as a Defective Drake: Snoweldon's Dragon

I then proceeded to roll, several times, like a car. I can remember a feeling of brief numbness by the time I finally stopped rolling. Then I felt like most of my skin had been ripped off, people started screaming, and I promptly blacked out.

And now I am here.

He's still not sure of what exactly he is. But the...egg yolk? The egg yolk is drying on him, and he can hear strange chirps coming from outside his egg. It is time to get out of here. Now having a somewhat better idea of what exactly is happening, he reaches out with his claws to start breaking off more pieces of his enclosure. He grunts in exertion but only hears a staticy warble peeter out of his mouth instead. Which makes sense considering that he has somehow been incarnated into an oddly albino lizard. Still, the sound surprises him enough for him to pause and give a few more scratchy, high pitched croons and chirps in curiosity. It's a bit odd, since lizards normally hiss. However, upon experimentation, he finds that he can hiss as well. Although when he does, he can feel something shift on the back of his neck and along his spine in specific places. Skin flaps, maybe? To show aggression?

At any rate, he can hiss aggressively like a lizard and chirp cheerily like a bird. What an odd lizard. Shaking his head, he returns to working his way through the egg. Normally, animals that hatch from an egg would have an egg tooth to help them, but he has no intention of putting his mouth anywhere

Reborn as a Defective Drake: Snoweldon's Dragon

near his egg shell. Just the thought of it makes his supposed skin flaps wiggle in disgust.

After a few more exhausting moments of punching through the egg shell, he finally makes a hole big enough to wiggle the upper half of his body out of the egg. For a moment, he finds the light absolutely blinding. Then, he feels his pupil contract, and he can see the inside of a large cave. To his right, the cave entrance stands tall and imposing as it lets in bountiful light from a noon-day sun. Bits of dried grass and hay are arranged about the cave in clumps. However, the sight of what he is sure are his sibling shocks him into silent awe and bewilderment.

He sees dragons rolling about the cave. They are large, tumbling creatures with too-short legs and big paws compared to their infantile bodies. Yet, even though these are clearly young, newly hatched reptiles, they still tower over him with dark, obsidian scales flecked with brighter reds, blues, and greens. Each dragon has a long, serpentine neck, four legs that are still too short for their bodies, a lengthy tail, and two wings sitting just behind their shoulders. Oddly enough, instead of horns, the little dragon can see skinny, sharply pointed ridges across the other dragons' bodies. These apparently help to convey emotions or signals as they seem to move about depending on the dragonet's mood.

The ridges look almost like the beginning of porcupine-shaped quills with oddly colorful stripes running horizontally

Reborn as a Defective Drake: Snoweldon's Dragon

in bands. The quills start at the top of the dragons' heads and create a deceptively fuzzy-looking head of quills. Another spoof of quills rises on their back, over their front shoulders in a very pointy approximation of a ruff. Similar smatterings of quills grow on the backs of their legs, on their rumps, and at the end of their tails.

He takes a moment to process what he's seeing. Even as he realizes that there are actual dragons in front of him, he still can't quite believe this is real. Perhaps, it is a dream while on his deathbed or maybe an effect of the knockout stuff used during surgery. He's not really sure, but either way, he really can't quite bring himself to look away from the dragonets in front of him.

All of them are primarily a dark, nearly black color with ash-grey underbellies and a single accent color incorporated in different patterns along their scales. A few are nearly entirely black but for red-colored throat scales and wing tips. Others have brightly-colored spines and cheetah spots from nose to tail tip. They are all, in a word, breathtaking.

So breathtaking, in fact, that when he hears an overly loud rumble shake the cave, he immediately ducks back in fright, only to realize that his 'mother' has just stood from her place towards the back of the cave and is heading towards the cave opening. She's a terrifying creature to behold. Standing at what must be a dozen yards high she fills the cave as much with her body as with her pure presence. Sharp quills from her shoulders and tail clack together like the warning of a rattlesnake.

While his siblings have soft looking baby ridges and small, chubby bodies, the mother of the brood is lithe and streamlined with powerful muscles, a gigantic wingspan, and a gracefully long, serpentine neck. Her quills rise thin and patterned from her scales, streaked in dark teal from tip to base. However, bits of red and brown remains litter the spikes and send a chill down his back. Whereas the other baby dragons look cute and immature, the mother dragon appears to be dangerous and deadly.

Before she leaves, she looks back towards the bundle of dragonets and gives a low, rumbling croon followed by a high pitched snort. He's not sure how, but he finds himself understanding the meaning instinctively.

Going for food. Stay here.

It's a bit basic as far as speech goes, but since dragons certainly don't have human vocal cords, he can understand the basic, uncomplicated language being a necessity. Still, he wants to bash his head against his eggshell at missing a chance at greeting his new mother. From what he can tell by looking at the empty, larger eggshells around him, he is either the last or one of the last to hatch. She has surely already been waiting a while for him. Although, it seems kind of odd how far away all the eggshells are from the actual nest and how close they sit to the cave opening? Wouldn't you put eggs in the nest until they

Reborn as a Defective Drake: Snoweldon's Dragon

hatched and only throw them out afterwards?

As it is, he ends up watching her exit the cave and jump into the air with a furious beating of wings instead of greeting her and telling her that he is, indeed, alive.

He hisses a warbling sigh of sorts before turning towards his brothers and sisters. They have returned to roughhousing with each other while being watched over by a larger dragon. The new dragon had come from the back of the cave and appears just as dark-scaled as his siblings. The dragon registers as female though he has no idea how he know that. Something about her red tipped quills being a darker red instead of a scarlet or highly saturated red? At any rate, he figures she might be one of his older siblings from a previous litter.

Ha-Thump!

He hoists himself out of his egg and onto the ground in an inelegant pile. He had meant to land and go over to his siblings, but he isn't used to four legs. These gangly limbs feel all sorts of weird when he tries to measure how far he needs to reach to touch the ground.

He huffs at the bruise he could already feel forming on his poor chest and tries to get his feet under him. First, he pushes upwards with his arms or front legs and ends up in an interesting sitting position.

So this is how dogs feel? Neat.

Then, he works on getting his shaking hind legs under him and pushing up. His body shakes with the effort but he steadies after a moment. Something soft pangs in his stomach, and he blinks as he realizes he's hungry. Maybe his siblings would have some food?

Walking is an interesting mix between extreme sports and a chore. When he tries to walk, he falls several times because he leaned too far to one side or the other. In the end, he is able to wobble towards his siblings a little ways before he gives up and just gives a loud croon for a hello.

Due to the noises made by the dragonets as they tussle about on the ground, only a few hear him, and the baby-sitting dragon misses his short call entirely.

Luckily, a soft-green-accented female, and two poison-blue-tipped males hear him and trot over in interest.

"What this?" the female chirps in curiosity. She tilts her head slightly, kind of like a bird, and he immediately wants to coo at how cute she is. He doesn't, but only because he doesn't know if cooing as a dragonet translates to an aggressive sound or something else.

"Smell brother. But...weak," one of the males hisses as he noses at the white dragon's wings and back.

"Weak," the other male agrees as he too nudges and sniffs.

Reborn as a Defective Drake: Snoweldon's Dragon

"*Hello,*" he chirps.

He doesn't really like how they seem to view him, but he still greets them excitedly. He can feel his wings fluttering atop him, and the wind on his tail tells him his tail is twitching as well.

At this point, a few of the other little dragonets have stopped their play and have come over to inspect him, drawing the attention of the babysitting female.

"*What?*" she calls over in a screechy bark.

"*Small, weak sibling,*" one of the numerous dragonets surrounding him calls back.

At this point, they have formed a semi-circle around him; the only way out is towards the cave entrance. He begins to feel a little claustrophobic, to be honest. But these are his siblings, and he won't begrudge them their infantile curiosity.

The babysitting dragon comes over with a series of loud, not-quite-rumbling steps and peers down at him with pinched eyes. Her lips form a snarl, and he can already tell what is about to happen is not going to be good. He forces himself back to his feet just as she takes a swipe at him with one of her claws.

She misses, but only just barely.

"*Weakling! Runt! Prey!*" she shrieks madly as she tries to bite him.

Again, she misses as he finally gets his feet under him to begin sprinting towards the cave opening. Strangely, running is easier than walking. Or perhaps that's just his adrenaline kicking in and guiding him in this strange new body.

Loud, raucous calls begin echoing from behind him, and it is with no small amount of terror that he realizes the babysitting dragon was not the only older juvenile dragon in the cave. She was just the only one watching the hatchlings. Loud thuds behind him tell him that the babysitter has run after him, and he just barely manages to roll to the side. Unfortunately, she doesn't entirely miss him this time, as one of her claws slices through the tip of his left wing.

He shrieks in pain and wails as he finally makes it out of the cave. Behind him, the babysitting female and her siblings are right on his tail and leave him no time to properly take in his surroundings. So instead of realizing he's on a cliff, he dives straight off of it.

And falls down. Down. Down.

And down.

Under the Sky... and through the Vale!

Thankfully, this new dragon body seems to have come with a set of instincts that provide helpful instructions on how to survive. Or at least, they would be helpful if he wasn't an infant trying to fly before his wings had even dried from the egg yolk.

Pain is the first thing he registers as he instinctively tries to open his wings. While dragons are not butterflies, their wing membranes are certainly very fragile when first hatched. Because his own wings haven't even been opened to allow proper blood flow or for the egg yolk to dry from his pearly scales. So when he tries to force them open, he ends up tearing strips of sensitive scales from his body. He opens them anyway, because feeling the wind rushing past him becomes a powerful motivator.

Unfortunately, his efforts don't actually stop his swift descent so much as change his downward plummeting to a sloped forward fall. He manages to glide, but not very well. It's a rushed and ragged descent, but he's not toppling front over end towards the ground. This, he counts as a very good thing.

Reborn as a Defective Drake: Snoweldon's Dragon

Now that he isn't plummeting towards certain death, the dragonet looks around and takes in the world he has dropped into.

Around him, the towering spires of red-and-cream-colored stone would have probably been something beautiful, like a fantasy video game or movie, but the dragonet can't find it within himself to admire them. His wings sting like liquid fire and the weight of his body on his newborn appendages feels akin to carrying a cement block rather than an undersized dragonet.

Spires of rough, sun-kissed stone rise into the sky. Caves and craggy ledges decorate the rock formations, and he can see other dark-scaled dragons perched upon them. Below him, a thick cloud layer obscures the ground at the base of the rocky spires.

Is he above the cloud layer? From here, he can see for miles; and looking up the dragonet shudders at the sight of a heavy, gaseous planet or moon taking up half the sky. Far away, a blazing star shines as this world's sun. Despite its brightness, the air is cool and crisp upon the white dragonet's wings, a testament to the high altitude the dragonet is falling through.

The heaviness of the dragonet's body doesn't feel good, and he can hear the raucous calls of his black-scaled siblings behind him. He needs to get out of here before their shrieks alert an adult. He doesn't quite know what about his white

Reborn as a Defective Drake: Snoweldon's Dragon

scales and smooth, edgeless horns set his siblings off, but he doesn't want to be on the receiving end of an adult dragon's wrath.

Consequently, he tries to angle his wings and hasten his descent. For a moment, he ends up actually slowing his descent and increasing the pain in his wings before he realizes that falling faster requires him to tilt his wings the *other* way.

Ah! That's how!

The shift takes effect immediately, and he almost panics when he begins approaching the cloud barrier at a breakneck pace.

Eep!

He shrieks a little when he hits the clouds. The cold shocks him, and the condensation gathers on his wings like a blanket of fresh frost. Against his better instincts, he finds himself closing his eyes against the icy droplets forming across his face. The chill does soothe his damaged wings though. The stinging feeling from where he had ripped the scales off dulls a little, and the edge that the babysitter dragon clawed numbs with the frigid air.

Yet, on the flip of a dime, he's out of the cloud layer, and hot, burning air superheats the water right off his face and wings. He opens his eyes with a start, and a warbling shriek slips from his maw in shock. Volcanic pits of brightly burning lava dot the land below him. Acrid fumes plume up like deadly flowers from dark lakes of burning tar, and the dragonet's eyes bulge as he flaps rapidly to swerve around one. Somehow, somehow his body knows how to swoop and swerve through the air instinctively and he narrowly avoids the superheated gas.

What... is this?

He had assumed the cloud layer was hiding green valleys or something, not a hellscape! Yet here in front of him, a massive lava lake bubbles between the rocky mesas that rise into the sky. Islands of dark stone litter the lake, and strange creatures plague both the lava and the space above it. He couldn't land here! He would never survive such a harsh environment. Where were the bountiful forests or sweet meadows that a little dragon like him needed to survive?

Gulping, the dragonet levels out his wings to try to extend his flight to at least past the lava lake. Luckily, the lava lake itself was on high ground with a river or superheated earth tumbling down a steep cliff up ahead. If he could at least glide past the falls, he would have more breathing room to find a place to land.

The dragonet blinks, and something clear flashes over his sight for a brief moment before sliding away.

Another membrane? he wonders shakily.

Nevertheless, it does relieve the stinging in his eyes enough for him to steady his glide a bit better.

The heat from the volcanic lake beneath him surges, causing the dragonet to nearly turn end over end as a strong

Reborn as a Defective Drake: Snoweldon's Dragon

wave of hot air hits his wings.

He flaps for perhaps the third time since stabilizing his gliding, and the action takes him soaring higher alongside his racing heartbeat. Forget taking off in a plane for the first time; this was the most terrifying, gravity-defying, aerial movement that the dragon had ever taken part in.

A loud, warbling shriek escapes from his mouth when the hot gust levels out and the added air pressure drops from beneath his wings, dropping him several feet down. Luckily, the loss in height is negligible; he's still several dozen yards above the lava lake; and the cliff side is approaching quickly. Again, he can't see what lies beyond the lake due to dark smog and smokey clouds, but anything is better than here, he thinks as he allows his gliding body to press into the hazy smog that guards the lava lake from the rest of the world.

Instantly, the white dragonet regrets it. The acrid taste of foulness fills his mouth, and he can practically feel grunge gathering across his body like putrid sludge. The raw patches of his wings burn and the cut on the tip of it stings fiercely. He coughs a short hacking cough, but that only invites the foul matter into his mouth. The smog feels disgusting, and his eyes, clenched shut as they are, tear up from the acrid fumes.

This must be what the death of the earth tastes like. There is no other thing that could ever taste as foul as this. Still, the smog barrier does not last forever, and soon cool, fresh air buffets his face like a gale.

Reborn as a Defective Drake: Snoweldon's Dragon

"Eeerk!" he shrieks as he opens his eyes to cool, snowy mountains and soft beds of green, springtime tundra.

What? Hadn't he just been in the heart of a volcano? How in the world did he end up in this icy wonderland?

Looking behind him, the dragonet only sees white, icy clouds covering a dark, foreboding cliff top. *Was all that smog really concealed by these puffy, icy clouds?*

The distinct sound of wing beats brings him out of his wonderings and back into the present.

"Kroo-AHHHH!" something roars in a loud, pitchy shriek.

Jerking, he looks up and feels his heart freeze at the sight of a large, scaly, draconic beast heading his way. It is colored similarly to the dragonet, white as snow. However, unlike the infant dragon, this creature has only a set of wings and hind legs. A long tail waves behind the creature in a mirror to its long, horned neck. In short, the dragonet had played enough video games in his past life to recognize a truly massive wyvern heading his way.

The tiny lizard's heart plummets further when he sees bright sparks light the creature's maw.

I am going to die here.

The fact is of no dispute. Yet, apparently, luck is rampaging against him today, as no sooner has he had the thought than another similar roar echoes across the snowy, mountainous landscape the dragonet has entered. Jerking his

Reborn as a Defective Drake: Snoweldon's Dragon

head around, the dragonet blinks just in time to see another wyvern launch itself from an ice ledge to his left and head his way. Panic truly begins to set in then, and he lets out a plaintive little wail as the two monsters speed towards him. Why does this sort of thing keep happening? Looking both ways, the little dragonet can tell that any sort of collision with these scaled giants won't turn out well for him.

Thinking quickly, he decides to stop, drop, and roll; dragonet style. Tucking his wings and lowering his head, the little dragon drops like a stone. Surprise washes over him at how quickly he was able to dive. Above him, the sound of the two wyverns colliding with a bang sends shockwaves bouncing around the icy canyon. Several snow drifts fall in soft thumps of noise, but he's honestly not too worried about the wyverns now. Instead, he's rather more worried about his continued freefall. Whimpering a little at the sight of the approaching ground, he tries to open his wings, but the pressure of the passing air keeps his wings plastered to his body.

He's only about a hundred yards from the ground when something bulldozes into him with a wild, cackling sound. Small, frigid claws scrape between his scales on his shoulder and draw thin rivulets of blood as icicle fangs pierce the side of his neck.

The dragonet chokes in shock, as he feels ice spreading through his arteries. A dying screech echoes from his throat as he frantically scrabbles to get away and to obtain a clear view

Reborn as a Defective Drake: Snoweldon's Dragon

of his aggressor. All he can see is a blurry image of red blood and snowy scales. Maybe some gray horns? Either way, pain still burns down the right side of his body when gravity reasserts itself and the creature's claws and jaws become the only thing keeping the dragonet in the air.

A half-strangled scream pulls itself from his throat as the creature rips through the tender scales on his shoulder due to the strain of holding his tiny body in the air. Unable to maintain its hold on his body, the predator's claws rip through the dragonet's soft scales before losing traction on his shoulder. When the beast's jaws become the only thing holding him in air, the dragonet can't help releasing a loud, high-pitched wail of pain. All of his body weight shifts to a small patch of muscle in his neck and the needle-sharp teeth impaling it. His neck lights up in intense, spiderwebbed strings of agony.

Reflexively, he desperately reaches his forelegs up to claw at what feels like a long, sinewy body. Something hot and wet coats his claws, and whatever is holding him jerks its teeth savagely while giving out a loud bark. The dragon sobs in a squeaky, shaking wail as more blood spills from his throat and due to the deepening hold of his enemy's fangs. Breathing becomes harder,, and if the creature squeezes too much tighter, it's going to puncture his airway or arteries, whichever is most prominent in this strange, draconic body.

Reborn as a Defective Drake: Snoweldon's Dragon

Again, he claws frantically at the creature holding him. This time, he really puts himself into it and manages to score a line of damage across what he thinks is the creature's head.

At any rate, whatever he hit must have been sensitive, as the dragonet finds himself released from the creature's grasp with a loud cry of pain from his aggressor.

Immediately, he flaps his wings and struggles away from the creature, only glancing back to see what looks like a winged, icey snake hovering in the air. Red claw marks dot the creature's side and a thick streak of blood covers the thing's eyes.

He had managed to blind it.

Good.

Viciousness burns down his throat just as hotly as his wounds. He does not like that thing or want it anywhere near him. *Let it be blinded for life and never bother him again.*

This in mind, he pushes past the heaviness of keeping himself in the air, the ongoing hunger that his newborn body has, and even the bright sparks of pain along his right side and wings. Right now, all that matters is finding somewhere safe. He can collapse then, and if not, he can always sleep when he's dead.

Probably.

He's not too sure what will happen if he dies again. Will he get to sleep then? Or will he just end up as a rabbit or something? Ehhh... he doesn't really want to die again, but it's neat to wonder at...

A sudden explosion of wind and heat behind him pulls the dragon out of his daydreams and sends him tumbling head over tail for a few moments before he can right himself with a few panicked wing strokes. The two wyverns from before are still duking it out further back into the canyon, and their clashes are the things of a kaiju movie more than actuality. Yet here, in this strange dream or actual reincarnation, their brawl shakes the mountains.

It's fearsome and awe-inspiring but frankly not where a little dragonet needs to be. With a frightened shiver, he hurriedly flaps away.

Similar to the hellscape he'd just left, the icy valley he's winging his way through continues to slope downward, away from the dragon's birthplace. Though he must have descended

Reborn as a Defective Drake: Snoweldon's Dragon

thousands of feet by now, the slope continues downward, becoming obscured by a white wall of mountain mist. How high did the towering, dragon-infested peaks soar? He doesn't know, but if his dragon body had not been meant for flying to great heights, the dragonet is certain that he would have been sick from altitude changes.

As it is, his wings ache with the strain of carrying far more than they should have at his age. Still, he pushes onward. The cold winds here are already too darn frigid for him, and he doesn't even want to think about what nightfall will feel like. He must find somewhere he can live before he hits the ground. Though he thinks he can probably fly for a little while longer under his own power now, the dragonet can tell just from how hard it is to direct his glide that he's not ready for long periods of extended flight.

Since he's technically not even a day old, to think that he can glide at all and cover so much ground is kind of crazy to begin with.

Thankfully, he's caught a tail wind that eggs him onwards, so he quickly finds himself approaching another barrier of thick, gaseous cover. Now that he's passed through two such barriers, he wonders what could be hidden on the other side. A desert? An oceanic land filled with sea monsters? He really doesn't know, but with the frigid wind pushing him onwards and the screams of the two wyverns echoing behind him, the dragonet has no choice but to continue forward. No

Reborn as a Defective Drake: Snoweldon's Dragon

matter what waits ahead, he will press on.

Taking a deep breath and closing his eyes tightly, the dragonet gives a great heave of his wings to push himself through the next cloud barrier.

This one, like the first, is cold. However, it is much, much colder than the first, and the dragonet cannot help giving a shrill cry as ice forms across his wings and tail. Sharp bits of what feel like hail strafe his sides. He registers a sharp rise in air pressure before he suddenly finds himself enveloped in warmer winds.

Blinking, he gasps as greenery glows in the light of the evening sun. Bright foliage lies thousands of feet beneath him, spread out like a canvas of tiny verdant speckles.

Glancing back, he catches sight of a massive mesa of dark stone rising from below. It towers above everything else in the area like an obsidian monolith. Yet, fog obscures its highest reaches. It is from that fog that he has just flown, and the dragonet can't repress the squeal of elation that passes from his jaws at the sight of the verdant, forest covered land below. He has done it!

True, he has no idea what he needs to eat as a newborn dragon, but at the very least, he is away from where he knows he cannot survive. Therefore, what comes next has to be easier than what has already happened, right?

He feels as if he has just jinxed himself.

As beautiful a sight as the green filled land below him is, the dragonet knows he cannot stay in the air forever. Ignoring his hunger and injuries, the dragonet lags, finding each wingbeat more onerous than the last. He doesn't think he has ever felt such a quickly growing exhaustion. Fatigue settles across his body like a wool blanket and burns through his muscles like the dying embers of a forge. He's also still bleeding sluggishly from his neck, and he doesn't know if dragon babies have all that much blood to lose. Human babies don't. He doesn't want to find out how similar dragon infants are to human ones.

He needs to land.

So, tucking his wings ever so slightly, the dragonet allows himself to angle towards the ground. He doesn't dive the way he did to flee the wyverns; he's learned better than to do that in this infantile body. But he definitely begins to descend.

The wind on his face and wings while seeing the ground speed past beneath him brings forth bubbles of exhilaration. Looking down, he can see giant trees that stretch high and wide speeding past him. They look like something from California's redwoods or perhaps a fantasy game. Thick, dark bark with dry, eldar bows reach towards the sky with viridian-green, heart-shaped leaves. Occasionally, the red cap of a giant mushroom peeks out from within the depths of the forest. It's truly beautiful from above, and the dragonet almost regrets his wings taking him lower and lower.

Eventually, he finds himself searching for a gap in the emergent layer and then the canopy as he comes within a few yards of the top layer of green growth. Flapping and coming to an abrupt decision, he halfway closes his wings and dives through a narrow gap in the canopy. Immediately, he finds himself squinting from a distinct lack of light. Beneath the top layer of trees, the shadows number more than the few sunbeams. Luckily, his eyes come equipped with a fast working pupil as he easily adjusts to the new lack of light.

Are his pupils thin like those of a cat's? It's certainly possible with how quickly his eyes adjusted. Either way, it's a question for another time, as the further downwards he drifts, the more branches he has to avoid.

Ducking, the dragon just manages to avoid a high branch, only to grab a mouth full of red berries instead.

"Pwah!" he croaks as he spits out a mixture of leaves and berries.

However, he isn't entirely upset, as the berries taste good, and he's hungry. Too bad he also ended up with leaves

Reborn as a Defective Drake: Snoweldon's Dragon

and bark. Mmm... berries though...

Taking a quick glance around, he spots more berries hanging from a branch to his left and snakes out his neck. One quick snap of his teeth, and he's holding a branch full of big, red berries.

Hum... He can't eat the berries now; he doesn't have hands to hold the stick and eat the ripe globs of sugary goodness. But when he lands...oh, when he lands! He's going to gobble them all up.

Of course, he's broken through the understory tree layer when he realizes that he doesn't have a clue how to land. And, even if he did, he isn't sure his shoulder will hold his weight with the dull burning he's been experiencing since passing the last cloud barrier.

Squeaking, he immediately begins to frantically flap his wings in an effort to ascend once more. Sadly, he can't rise on stifling updrafts so near the forest floor here. All of the air feels cool and moist. It drapes heavily on his wings, and though he struggles to rise, he can't seem to fight past the thick layer of moisture in the air.

As the space between the forest floor and his struggling form decreases, he comes to the certainty that he's going to have to land whether he knows how or not. Taking a gulp, he grits his teeth around his stolen berry branch and stretches out his uninjured leg.

Back when he was a kid and human, he'd seen a few martial art shows and displays so he knew that you should never fall from a great height without diffusing the kinetic force in some way.

Most falls have the user rolling with the force and coming up afterwards. The dragonet has never seen someone use a fall technique going so fast, but heis sure the same rules apply here.

Too quickly, he makes contact with the ground. From there, the world passes in a blur of motion as he tucks his wings, legs, tail, and head close to his body in as close a mimicry to a bowling ball as he can. Somehow, this works in protecting him from going splat against the earth.

However, tucking into a ball does not stop him from careening forward head over tail in a dizzying rush of colors. With a thud, he collides against the spongy side of a large, blue chunk of fungus.

Blinking, he watches the world spin without his permission for a few minutes. That landing was rough. Rolling over and over like that sent both his stomach and his head for a loop, and the harsh stop via fungus didn't help with that. Though, he is infinitely grateful that he had hit something softer than the hardwoods surrounding him. If he had hit one of the giant trees, he might have actually gone splat like a pancake.

Moving his head gingerly, he takes in his upside-down surroundings before slowly maneuvering his aching body to lie flat along the ground instead of upside down against the fungus. Most of the undergrowth here consists of ferns ranging from normal-sized leafy plants that were about as big as he was to gigantic examples of megafauna that had to be at least fifteen yards high. In between the fibrous stalks of ferns, he can see thick trunks and root systems for the giant trees. Most of the trees have roots bigger around than an eighteen wheeler, and the less he thinks about the truly ridiculous size of the actual trunks, the better. Giant mushrooms and strange colored weeds dot the area around him in differing hues of red, purple, and even blue. At any rate, the dragonet is at least relieved to see no carnivorous beasts in his immediate area.

Whining slightly, he turns onto his stomach and winces as a sharp twinge runs through his injured shoulder. Arching his neck carefully, he looks down at the damage done to his tiny self.

Red, jagged lines run across his shoulder from where the creature's claws had ripped through his skin and muscles. It bleeds sluggishly, though the edges have already begun clotting. Hopefully, the rest will clot soon despite the depth of the wound. Meanwhile, his neck has already begun clotting. Despite the depth of the punctures, the actual surface area affected isn't all that large due to the needle-like nature of the ice serpent's teeth. He only has a few spots of dark, clotted blood to account for the deeper ache he can feel closer to his esophagus. Hopefully he doesn't have any internal damage. He doesn't know if he even has a way to fix something like that.

Reborn as a Defective Drake: Snoweldon's Dragon

Still... at least he's alive? He's pretty sure he's alive. No death-bed hallucination can hurt this badly. He's definitely going to be feeling it for a few days. Groaning a strange, breathy sort of rumble, he slowly moves to stand.

Wobbling, he places most of his weight on his other three legs rather than his injured one. Just from looking at it and feeling the throbbing from it tells him that walking on that leg is a bad idea. So...he sort of hop-wobble-waddles over to where his branch of berries have fallen. A few berries have fallen off, likely in his mad snowball landing, but most of them are still there.

Drooling slightly, he sets himself gingerly onto his haunches and then back down to lying on his belly. Then he digs in.

These berries are without a doubt some of the sweetest things he has ever tasted. Their little seeds make pleasing sounds as he crunches down on them, and the juice dribbles out of his mouth and down his snout. He can't bring himself to slow down though. His stomach rumbles fiercely with infantile hunger, and he is but a slave to its demands. Ravishing, frantic urgency thrums in his veins now that he finally has food in front of him.

Loathe as he is to admit it, he probably consumes the berries like the wild predator he resembles. He doesn't really know, as the next thing the dragonet is aware of is licking his chops, a barren branch, and his own strange, cooing purr that

Reborn as a Defective Drake: Snoweldon's Dragon

bumbles from the back of his throat.

Ah, that was good.

He blinks once, twice, and immediately decides it's time for a nap. All that running--or flying--for his life has left him in an exhausted stupor. Struggling back onto his non-injured legs, he looks around for somewhere to rest.

He's not seen anything that would want to eat him yet, but he's sure there's something here that wouldn't mind a baby-dragon-sized snack. He's certainly not going to make it easy for them by falling asleep out in the open.

But... where can he hide? He's too small to climb the massive trees above him. Their lowest branches are a good twenty yards in the air. The foliage is dense, but his scales gleam a bright white even in the dim shadows of the bottom layer of the forest. He needs to find somewhere no one can see him, like a baby-dragon-sized burrow or something.

Turning about, he wobbles over to one of the colossal roots. If there isn't a dragon-sized hiding place, he'll just have to make one. Yet, he pauses as he realizes that he can't possibly dig with one of his front legs so injured. Snorting in disappointment, he's about to turn away when an idea hits him. He's not just a dragon, so why is he acting like one? He's a human, and humans use tools. He still can't dig with one front leg, but perhaps he doesn't need to.

He moves slowly over to a group of giant stalks and looks up at their wide, circular leaf heads. Oddly enough, these

Reborn as a Defective Drake: Snoweldon's Dragon

look just like dollar weeds from down the southern coast if you discount the weird blue coloring and purple spots. Huffing at the absurdity, he bites through a few of the stalks and drags them over to the corner where the root meets the tree trunk. There, he lowers himself to the ground and slices thin cuts through certain parts of the dollarweed leaves with his claws. Then, he begins weaving them together to form a strange, dollar-weed-made camouflage tarp. It's honestly pretty bizarre looking with its neon purple and blue coloring, but it should hide him. And he's so tired. His body trembles as he pulls the camouflage weave over his head. He drifts off as soon as he rests his head back down on the ground.

If this is what being a dragon is like...it's honestly not that great. He prefers being a human named Isaac.

· · · · ·

The earth shaking wakes him. The light hasn't changed from its strange gloom, so he assumes he either slept through the night or that he hasn't slept very long at all. It's honestly a little bewildering not to be able to judge time by the sky.

Still, he has very little time to notice that before the ground shakes again. Going wide eyed, he sits as still as he can under his camouflage when the earth shakes again. He's seen way too many scary dinosaur movies to ignore the sound of something truly massive exerting its weight on the earth.

Reborn as a Defective Drake: Snoweldon's Dragon

Displaced air rattles his camouflage. Oh, sweet nevermore, the creature must be huge. Shifting ever so slightly, he peaks through the holes in his covering. What awaits him is both awe inspiring and petrifying.

Massive, tree-trunk-sized legs lead up to a broad-chested body of what has to be the most demonic-looking chicken in existence. Really, the basic shape is the same. The creature has an almost comically proportioned head and neck sitting atop a full chest, two small wings, and skinny bird feet. The bird's feet are about as big around as the trees nearby, and its body must be bigger than a large house. Of course, instead of feathers, the creature is covered with sharp, oddly-colored rock and crystal. Most of these run comparatively short along the underbelly and the legs with soft blue light dancing in the crystals. However, along the creature's spine, blood-red crystals point skywards in jagged clumps of bright color before ending in a burnt-orange tuft at the rear of the beast.

The same burnt-orange paints a line of crystals from an obsidian beak to the junction of the creature's neck and back. Dark pits rest where the eyes should have been, and a single smoldering-red iris is the only clue as to where the gigantuan beast is looking. The eyes gaze murderously at something other than the dragonet, thankfully.

Still, it feels as if he can hardly bear to breathe as another massive foot shakes the earth with a monstrous step. The creature walks forward slowly and stills for a few moments.

Reborn as a Defective Drake: Snoweldon's Dragon

It's looking at something with a half cocked head, peering poisonously through the megaflora.

The dragonet blinks, and in the span of that blink, the mega-chicken moves. There's a thundering of steps, and a rabbit with horns and a tail made of leaves bursts from a nearby fern. It's much bigger than the dragonet but not even a quarter of the size of the monster chicken.

"**RaaaAAAAWOAKKKKKK!**" The chicken begins with a low growl that quickly grows to a deafening shriek.

Then, to the astonishment of the dragonet, the demonic creature's chest cavity begins opening to reveal its insides. He can't see much from where he is positioned, but he thinks he can make out the intestines and lungs from within the bloody, fluid-covered mess. At the crescendo of the beast's screech, the stomach suddenly detaches from what the dragonet supposes is the esophagus, shooting out so quickly the dragonet sees afterimages. He can't see where the rabbit has fled from his hiding spot, but the sharp cry and crunch of flesh and bones leave no illusion for the dragonic infant in regards to the smaller creature's fate.

Squelching, wet noises fill the forest. Ducking, the
dragonet squeezes his eyes shut as he hears the slithering
noise of the monster chicken retracting its stomach. He doesn't
look back up when something wet splatters on the forest floor.
If he did look, he's pretty sure he'd start retching, and he
doesn't want to attract the attention of such an aggressive fowl.

After several hair-raising moments of horror-movie
sounds, the ground shakes with a muted boom. Another loud
footstep follows the first. The evil chicken is moving away, and
the draconic child couldn't feel happier about it. Finally, when
he can barely hear the thunderous footsteps of the monster,
the dragonet raises his head.

Once more, the gloom of the bottom-most portion of the
forest greets him. It looks as peaceful as it did before he went
to sleep, but now the sight only fills him with paranoia. He

Reborn as a Defective Drake: Snoweldon's Dragon

should have kept flying. Really. This place was so very, very, very not safe!

He ducks his head with a whine and buries it between his front paws. There is no way he could live here with such dangerous creatures around. He is likely lucky the stupid chicken didn't pick up on the smell of his own blood. The little dragon feels the itchy sensation of dried blood across his shoulder and neck even now.

Panic thuds low in his heart and chest as he takes a deep inhale and scents the metallic tang of blood. He needs a bath before something with better senses comes along and decides to gobble him up. Raising his head back up, he glances over his shoulder and spies the thick scab that has formed over the claw marks from yesterday. Losing more blood would make him weak, but he doesn't plan on using that leg for a while anyway. As long as he's careful, he should be able to hobble about without reopening the wound.

Peeking out of his camo tarp, the little dragon doesn't see anything moving. Instead, the quiet murky trees and strangely luminous mushrooms greet his eyes. It looks safe.

Taking a sniff, he grimaces as the smell of his own blood overwhelms almost everything else. He twitches his wings in irritation only to grimace at the soreness he feels there. It's a good thing he doesn't intend to fly; yesterday's exercise has left him quite sore.

Hoisting himself onto his three uninjured feet, the dragonet slithers out from under his camo tarp. He thinks about folding it and carrying it with him in his mouth, but the wilting leaves and discoloration dotting the broken flora would probably be almost as bad as no cover at all. It wasn't hard to make, so he leaves it beside the massive roots of the tree he slept under.

Water would typically gather at low places, right? Glancing around, he determines that off to his right might be slightly lower than off to his left. Perhaps. If he was lucky... Okay, he was really just making a guess. But a guesstimate is better than doing nothing, so off he goes.

It's awkward, this wobbling forward on three legs. Every few moments, he tips forward and has to flap his wings rapidly to keep from face-planting into the leaf litter coating the forest floor. The actions pull at his stiff muscles, but he is unwilling to learn what the dirt and decaying leaf matter here tastes like. Therefore, he determinedly shuffles onward. Every now and then, the dragonet pauses to take in the noises of the forest around him, but the tranquil, murky forest is all he can sense. It's a little nerve racking, being unable to sense any life at all. For all he knows, there could be a hungry predator sleeping nearby, waiting for the sound of delicious prey to wake it from its nest.

Luckily, no hungry monster cats jump down from the leafy boughs above. His trek forward is largely quiet; only his own stumbling footsteps and hasty wing flaps betray his presence. All the same, when he loops around a fifty foot tree trunk to see glimmering, watery light reflected onto the tree trunks ahead, he can't help but feel relief.

Water. Finally.

Except, when the dragonet crests the small ridge overlooking the shimmering light source, what he sees isn't actually very water-like. A silky, shimmering liquid rests in a shallow hollow. The color is something between a pearl's creamy coat and a diamond's stark white interior. The pool of liquid glitters like a diamond too. It's mesmerizing with its shiny exterior, and he's struck with the overwhelming urge to go touch it. Even though it takes up all of the space of a puddle, it moves from side to side hypnotically and thickly like oil.

Still... he doesn't know what it is and can't approach it too brashly. Giant chicken monsters aside, he doesn't know enough about this new land to ascertain whether or not the liquid is safe. So... he stealthily approaches the pond of mystery fluid.

Or, as stealthily as a three-legged baby dragon can. At any rate, nothing pops up to attack him before he reaches the edge of the puddle-sized anomaly. Peering into it, he wonders at the lack of even a shadow on the silvery liquid. Despite leaning over it with his new draconic neck, he can't see even the slightest hint of shadow thrown onto it. Rather, the liquid remains brightly colored, as if lit from some interior source. Curious, he feels the strongest urge to touch it.

It doesn't smell dangerous. Or at least, he doesn't think it does, as he still can't smell much over the scent of his own dried blood. Surely though... one little touch can't hurt?

The silvery mixture swirls enticingly as he lowers his head down toward it.

A moment is all it takes. Just the very tip of his snout brushes the pool, but that's enough for it to react. As soon as his snout causes ripples to form across the top of the liquid, it moves in a whirlwind of bright, diamond colored droplets and streams in a blinding, strobe-light effect. Yet, he can't look away. Whatever force pulled him to touch the puddle-sized aberration still holds sway over his body.

Instead, he stares fixedly at a million bright, glimmering droplets that have filled the air around him and around the pool. Unlike before, these tiny floating treasures glow in the exuberant shades of the rainbow. Blue, green, red, yellow, orange, pink, purple, teal, and so many more shades of the world dazzle his eyes. Below him, the pool glows brightly,

Reborn as a Defective Drake: Snoweldon's Dragon

casting radiant beams of light into the world. The figments of light bathe the dragonet in something hot and burning. He clenches his eyes shut at the heat that washes over his body. As a dragon, he should be protected from mere fire and heat. He had been entirely fine floating above the lava pits beneath his birth place. A little uncomfortable, but not truly hurt by the heat.

Now, he somehow feels more than a mere physical heat as it lathers his frame in intense pain. The heat centers upon his chest, over where he thinks his heart is and he almost gags in response. Cracking his eyes open, he's just in time to see bright tendrils of light reaching to drag him into the pool and all the little motes of color flash a bright, warning yellow. And then, he's pulled into the pool and sees no more.

Waking at all is unexpected. Or at least it is later, when he's had a chance to think about it. At first, however, all he collects of his surroundings is a soft gentle heat across the back of his body. Sunlight. It feels soft and loving compared to the harsh heat of before.

For a moment, he allows himself to languish there, unwilling to contemplate more than the soft heather clumped around and beneath his body. Then, true recollection of his last few thoughts dance across his mind's eye, and he bolts upright.

Heart jackhammering in his chest, the dragonet stares uncomprehendingly at the open field of soft grasses. He's...in a field. In the daylight. Just...sitting in the grass.

Looking about, he sees that he's not about to be devoured by sentient silver liquid or sucked into some sort of rainbow quicksand. He's alive, as his beating heart dictates to him. It's surreal and unprecedented, but the little dragon certainly isn't about to start complaining. Instead, he chooses to take stock of his surroundings.

Blinking at the bright light, the dragonet peers about and takes in his new surroundings. The field sits surrounded by tall, thick pine trees with dark needles and rough-looking bark. Bees and small insects buzz in and out of the forest. They work merrily at collecting pollen from the many brightly-colored flowers within the field. To the dragonet's shock, a mother doe and her fawn graze peacefully a few yards away from him. Both of them tower above him and feed happily on the sweet grasses. They appear to be either unaware of the infant dragon's presence or uncaring. He chuffles softly as the fawn reaches up to nuzzle her mother in care. Such... cuteness...

Even someone like himself is not immune.

Still, such peace can never last and the sound of harsh, graceless footfalls reaches the clearing. Immediately, the mother deer and her fawn bolt in the dragonet's direction. For a moment, he thinks he's going to be trampled by mere happenstance and ducks his head until his body lies flush against the ground. A soft breeze drifting across his nose is the only sensation he feels, and he opens his eyes just in time to perceive the last hoof of the fawn as she follows her mother's example in hopping over him.

They had apparently known he was there all along.

Rustling at the opposite side of the clearing alerts the baby dragon of newcomers. In response, he wedges himself under a mound of heather and into the soft, moist dirt below. It spreads sickeningly across his scales, slimy and cold where the sun was hot and soothing. He paws at the dirt on his nose and manages to rub it off, but the rest cloaks him uncomfortably.

Reborn as a Defective Drake: Snoweldon's Dragon

He really could use a bath at this point.

The crunch of lush grass blades beneath a boot draws his eyes to the edge of the clearing where a silver silhouette walks out of the trees.

Well maintained, glittering chainmail bends over a human form as it enters the clearing. To the dragonet, the harsh, reflective metal used as a breastplate and helmet seems to radiate strength. The sash bearing what seems to be a purple-and-gold coat of arms sways slightly from its place at the knight's waist. A sword wavers in the knight's right hand, and a shield rests on the left forearm.

The situation feels like something unreal: a story, fable, or legend. Yet, as the first enters the clearing, so does a second. Then, a third. And then, a fourth.

In total, four knights step into the clearing with the dragonet. Each bears the same design on his or her coat of arms and each wears glimmering chainmail and steel armor.

Then, from behind the knights step two purple-robed humans: a man and a woman. Their robes bear identical

Reborn as a Defective Drake: Snoweldon's Dragon

designs with gold-thread embroidered hems, long, flowing sleeves, and a line of golden buttons along the right side to hold it closed. Around their waists, steel cords give security to various sized leather bags and pouches while a light blue hooded shawl covers their heads. The two wear the coat of arms across their left breast, and each carries a long staff of some sort. The man's staff twists about in a strange, root like fashion while the woman's blue staff resembles a rod of unknown make with a reflective gemstone at one end. Despite not having a noticeable sharp point, the man and woman treat their staffs like weapons, all military discipline and careful, subconscious training. Perhaps they used them as blunt weapons?

Though they don't appear sturdy enough for that...

Any other potential pondering grinds to a halt when the first knight stops a third of the way into the clearing. He looks around as if searching for something, Then, he speaks, and the dragonet, both surprised and grateful, somehow understands the language because the noises coming out of the man's mouth are not English.

Can dragons speak all tongues, or was this just a strange happenstance due to reincarnation? Either way, gratitude floods the little dragon's mind. The words the knight utters, do not.

"I don't see anything." Turning, the knight looks back towards the two-purple robed individuals. "Are you sure this is the right place?"

"Yes," The woman answers in a sharp voice. "This is where we sensed the void magic. Perhaps it has run off? You knights took far too long to gather your armor and get out here. It's been hours since we sensed the anomaly."

She looks about and sniffs haughtily at the green, flower-covered clearing.

"Oh, it's our fault now? You're the one who couldn't wait for us to get our horses ready. If you had let us saddle up, we could have been here ages ago," the knight growls back to the woman as he swings around to face her.

The armor gleams like a beacon in the sunlight, and the baby dragon can't help but admire it. It looks so cool! Like a knight straight out of an RPG or fantasy novel. Not to mention, its shimmering surface calls to the instinctive part of his mind. He really wants to touch it and maybe even fall asleep on it. How warm it would be from the sun's bright rays!

"Please! With how long you take to get ready we would've lost even more time. Everyone knows the knights of Cavadeer care more for looks than actually doing their jobs." This time, the male robed figure speaks. His voice wavers oddly in a strange almost rhythmic way. Is he speaking in some sort of cadence?

"Oh, like you and your mages are any better, Tain. You take so long to set up your silly little spells and wards that any real fighting's done before you robed fellows get to the battlefield." Another knight, the third one this time, speaks up. His voice leans on the edge of excitement and amusement, and for all that the situation radiates tension, he seems more entertained than anything. The little dragon also notes that despite wearing the same uniform as the other knights, his armor carries with it a carefree attitude due to how sloppy it looks in comparison. Whereas the other knights have all carefully cleaned and cared for their armor, this knight's armor is dirty, scratched, and even a little dented in places. His long, blonde hair also cascades wildly down his back in sharp contrast to his comrade's carefully braided or short hair. Overall, his appearance incites a sense of disconnect between himself and his fellow knights.

At the man's words, the two 'mages' straighten and self-importantly puff out their chests.

"Why you-" The woman begins to rage only to be cut off by a final knight appearing from within the tree.

"I do believe that's quite enough from the lot of you," the new knight growls in a voice cracked by age and irritability.

This knight carries himself differently from the rest with slow, ponderous steps, his age lines his form in worshipful experience and veneration. A gray, curly beard trails down his chest in a wave. Just as the other knights, he wears steel-bright armor with purple cloth to display the golden crest. Similarly to the blonde knight's armor, the old man's armor has several scratches and dents. However, the shining surface and carefully buffed scratches speak of diligent maintenance. Another difference between this new knight and the others is a bright purple feather at the top of his helm. Due to the man's age, the dragonet wonders if this is a distinction due to a difference in rank. Probably, the little lizard concludes, eyeing the man's commanding posture and tone.

"Honestly, I send you lot off to scout ahead, and I find you bickering and belittling each other," the man huffs before surveying the field. "You are correct in that there is no monster here, though I wonder if it was here to begin with."

He finishes his statement by unhooking a flask of something from his hip and taking a long swig of it. Clearly, he's not concerned for either his image or his surroundings. Meanwhile, the mages appear to become even more offended and agitated.

"Captain Snovalen, I assure you this is the place indicated by our scrying team. The rift occurred here." Tain defends his fellow mages indignantly.

"I'm sure it did, Mage Tain. However, even if a rift occurred here, that doesn't mean a monster stepped through. Sometimes large or powerful monsters can peer through or simply not fit through a rift. Just because a rift opened here, it doesn't mean something crossed over. In fact, I surmised from the beginning when the scrying mages first sensed such a large release of mana that we were dealing with a monster peeking through instead of a crossover. The pristine state of this

Reborn as a Defective Drake: Snoweldon's Dragon

clearing confirms it." Here, Captain Snovalen gestures out to the green clearing. "If something of the power that was sensed were to cross over here, this clearing and the surrounding area would no longer exist. The scrying team reported at least a class five monster. That indicates a creature from the Hellcaster realm, if not the Starpeaks realm." Here, the captain pauses as his fellow warriors and mages make startled, gasping noises.

The dragonet blinks and tilts his head curiously. It hadn't taken much to realize that the monster the group is searching for is himself. Even though modern literature may paint dragons in interesting shades of morality, most ancient stories clearly depicted dragons as monstrous beasts or villains. Judging by their knightly and fantasy-themed clothes, the dragonet can assume the group comes from a more traditional or less advanced civilization. Thus, they could potentially see dragons as a threat. Furthermore, his own circumstances add evidence to the assumption.

Somehow, the puddle he can remember touching transported him here instead of eating him, and this group of warriors and magic users had sensed his arrival. But apparently, they think he should be big enough to destroy this whole area judging by the amount of magic or whatever? Does he even have magic? He's... not sure. The little dragon doesn't feel very magical, but he also doesn't feel as weird as he thinks being reborn as a dragon should feel. Or maybe he just doesn't

Reborn as a Defective Drake: Snoweldon's Dragon

notice it because his new body is used to being magical? Still...he really doubts he could destroy a whole clearing.

His mother probably could though...and the names they were using did kind of sound like two of the places he had flown through. Hellcaster sounded like it could relate to the area with the lava lake he had flown through yesterday, and Starpeaks could probably be used to describe his birthplace at night. Being so high up, the craggy peaks of his birth family's nesting grounds likely had an absolutely gorgeous view of the night sky. So these knights could then be assumed to be looking for him.

Somehow, that thought doesn't exactly give him the warm and fuzzies. The swords, shields, and even the mages' staffs seem to glimmer dangerously at him now that he has realized the humans' presumably dangerous intentions towards himself. Still, time moves on as Captain Snovalen continues with his explanation after his subordinates absorb his previous statement. All of them are a good bit paler judging by the small bit of them exposed to the little dragon's sight.

"As you can imagine, any beast crossing over from those realms would be catastrophic to this area. Yet, not even a blade of grass has been disturbed unduly in this area. Therefore, it can be assumed that nothing passed through the rift this time." Snovalen points to the grass covering the clearing before looking back at his subordinates.

"Also, if a creature of that sort of power had crossed

Reborn as a Defective Drake: Snoweldon's Dragon

over, regardless of size or the distance from here to the Snoweldon fortress, we all would most certainly know it. Such a beast's very existence disturbs and unbalances the natural order. Each of its breaths would exude more raw mana than any holy site or magic rite in existence. It would create a miasma of thick mana around itself. Due to the density of it, everything in its immediate area would die from hyper-mana saturation. This creates what is essentially both a dead zone of all life, and a beacon for mages and magic knights alike. We would have definitely sensed its oppressive power from back in the fort if something from the Hellcaster realm or higher decided to pay us a visit." Snovalen finishes his lecture with a sure nod and another glance around the clearing.

The little dragon resists ducking closer to the wet earth he is hiding on but only because he's not sure the movement wouldn't attract the man's eyes. Going by how Snovalen doesn't seem to like anything from the realms the dragonet has traveled through, he's not exactly in a rush to announce his presence.

"Then why did we march all the way out here, sir?" One of the knights pipes up in curious belligerence. Surprisingly, the voice is female, though the little dragon can see no distinction in either shape or uniform. She looks just like the other knights; it's just that her voice rings with a clearly woman-like pitch. Maybe there's extra padding on the inside of the armor to give it the same shape and distribution of weight?

Reborn as a Defective Drake: Snoweldon's Dragon

"Because it's our duty to check every potential crossing, and I wanted a look at Snoweldon's newest recruits. I have to say, the academy sure knows how to churn out empty helmets. You lot are even worse than last year's batch at being thoughtless, and that's hard to do." The captain gives the lot a dark, dead-eyed look that has a few of the group shrinking into themselves.

The others puff up in offense to his words, but the little dragon just thinks they look like angry peacocks when they do that.

"Captain Sno-" The first knight starts off, his shoulders stiffening in outrage.

The dragonet thinks he can see the man's darker eyebrows come together into a sharp point. Thankfully, the knight captain cuts him off before he can properly get started though.

"Sir Camuel," Snovalen all but growls.

Camuel falls silent, apparently unable to argue with the old captain when he uses such a dark tone. The dragonet can't blame him. It had almost felt as if there was some sort of pressure placed on him when the captain had spoken, and the baby dragon wasn't even the recipient of such a rebuke. He can't imagine what being the recipient of such would feel like, but judging from the subtle rattling he can hear in the breeze, not well.

"All of you." And now, the aged warrior turns his icy

gaze onto the rest of the knights and the mages. "You've disappointed me greatly. You are fresh from the academy. You should not have such deep seated bias against the people who work on keeping you alive while serving Cavadeer. Mages *and* knights exist to protect and serve directly in the line of fire. While you cast your spell work, who do you think is keeping monsters from jumping down your throat?"

Here, the mages look vaguely guilty or perhaps unsettled as they avoid Snovalen's gaze. Meanwhile, the knights grin and elbow each other. Clearly, they thought they were going to be getting off scott-free.

"Knights, who do you think heals you and lets you get back to your families at the end of the day? Or lends you their magic to increase your attack power? Or binds the monster so you can strike it? All you do is hit things with pointy bits of steel, they're the ones who make what you do relevant." Captain Snovalen finishes his chastisement with a blusterous sigh.

"Honestly, this squabbling is both immature and a shame to your honor. Regardless of whether you lift a sword or a focus, these are your brothers and sisters in arms, and they deserve your respect for defending the country at your side. Now, come along. We might as well break for the noontide meal before heading back to Snoweldon."

And with those words, Captain Snovalen whistles sharply with two fingers stuck in his mouth. A whinny sounds out from the trees, and the dragonet watches in awe as several horses trot into the clearing. The creatures are tall and stocky with lots of fluffy fur around their hoofs. Even the fur along their back seems thicker than usual and their manes hang heavier with the weight of tightly braided hair. All but one sport the same brown and white stocking coloring. The odd one out wears a golden coat and winnies happily as she trots over to Captain Snovalen. The dragonet blinks at it, as even though he was never a horse fanatic, he had certainly never seen a gold clydesdale before. Maybe it was just something to expect of this world?

Either way, the little dragon loses his train of thought when the captain starts rooting through the packs to pull out tightly-packaged bundles. Just from the smell alone, he can tell what those packages contain.

Meat! he thinks with joy.

The savory, salty scent of dried ham and pork reaches out to him tantalizingly, and he finds himself unable to sit still as the mages and knights gather round for their meal. Carefully but doggedly, he crawls through the heather towards the knights. His stomach practically begs him to move forward, and with each tiny dragon-length closer he moves, his mouth waters more and more. The scent of such a delicious banquet drowns out his common sense and sense of preservation.

As he approaches, the little dragon can see his target. The burlap sack containing the meat has been laid just behind

Captain Snovalen, still partially open. By this point, due to his slow pace, the knights and mages have drifted into somewhat jilted but steady conversation as they focus on consuming their meals. This is his chance. If he can just remain unnoticed, he can steal some of that delicious, lovely, divine meat for himself. A burst of surprised laughter blossoms among the circle of men and women and he takes his chance. Using his claws, the little dragon hooks himself to the burlap sack and wiggles his way inside. His shoulder twinges badly, but with the sweet chance of meat so close, the little dragon hardly pays it any mind.

Instead, the only thing on his mind is the plump feeling beneath his body and flesh sliding in between his claws. Wiggling a little to the side so that he's farther away from the opening, the dragonet takes a pull of meat with his sharp infant teeth and chokes it down. For his past self, it likely would have been pretty disgusting, but the little dragon can barely contain his croon of delight at the feeling of meat puffing out his neck and then slowly inching down to his stomach. Emboldened, he rips another chunk off before swallowing that piece down whole, too. The feeling is so good that he repeats it a third time. And then again. And Again. And many more times until he's feeling a little too stuffed and until a comparatively large section of the pork is missing.

Ahhh.... He thinks to himself in contentment.

A yawn bubbles up and out of his mouth. He's... actually feeling pretty drowsy now...

Reborn as a Defective Drake: Snoweldon's Dragon

Before he knows it, his eyes have slipped closed and his consciousness has fled into the skies above.

The next thing the dragon feels is a steady rocking motion from side to side. The burlap sack is pulled taut against his scales, and his body is squished somewhat uncomfortably between the remaining chunk of meat and the rough fabric. He blinks bewilderedly before the muted clip-clop of a horse's hooves and rocking of the sack finally clue him in to the need to wake fully.

Looking up, he can spy some muted light shifting through the top of the sack, though the draw strings are now pulled tight. Wiggling, the little dragon scrambles up on top of the meat using his claws. Then he carefully peers through the small hole at the top.

Dark, green covered boughs sway gently above, and he can see the soft brown fur of a horse's coat to the side. Ahead, the beast's massive head peers forward at the behest of the rider, who sits tall and looming. Again, the dragonet is surprised at just how small he is in comparison to everything around him. Truly, he could fit in a grown man's hand with room to spare!

At any rate, he's seen enough to bob his head back down

in the sack. It would not be good if the knight found him in the meat sack. Still, with nothing else to do, the dragonet surprises himself by chomping down on some more of the meat. Somehow, he's hungry again, despite eating only a few hours ago. He supposes it must be due to being a baby dragon. Maybe he needs the energy to grow? He doesn't feel like he's been growing but maybe he will soon? At any rate, the meat tastes good with salty proteins and scrumptious texture. Judging by everyone's clothes, he's currently in a medieval period where they dry their food and salt it to keep it from spoiling.

He might tire of it eventually, but for now he's going to enjoy this salty tang.

Mmmm...

He nibbles on the meat on and off as the contingent of knights make their way home slowly. Occasionally, he can hear them chatting between themselves, but for the most part, a silence presides over the group. He can't tell if it's an awkward or comfortable silence from his place in the sack, but he supposes it can go either way. The old captain, Snovalen, seemed like the sort to keep things calm and comfortable, but the fighting between the mages and knights before his intervention had displayed clear tensions between the new knights and the new mages. Sighing, the dragon continues to munch away as the afternoon light begins to wane and the birds begin to quiet.

Finally, the soft thumps of horses trotting through the

wilderness changes to the sharp clip-clop of hooves and horse shoes on stone, and the dragon perks up. As he peaks through the top of the bag again, a shadow passes over the group. Looking up, he's just in time to see the brick patterns of a portcullis pass by. It's an old thing by the looks, but no less impressive with its fifty foot high walls and iron gate. Individuals dressed in significantly more leather versions of the knights' armor man the gate and seem to be inspecting a long line of visitors. The little dragon supposes those must be regular foot soldiers; warriors serving the existing government but not part of the aristocracy.

A long line of people extends out of the gate. Covered wagons drawn by large oxen, horse-drawn carts, and even a few people on foot stand in the area outside the gate as they await their own turn to pass through.

On the other side of the wall, tall, two or three story buildings rise into the sky. Most of these are made of dark colored wood, with murky, poor quality glass windows and mix-matched patch ups here and there. These townhouses are clearly where the less prosperous dwell. It's a startling difference to the knights' own splendor and high quality garments. The people here match their houses too. They wear rough, homespun cloth and simple, easy to dye colors. Some wear furs, and the dragon wonders what time of year it is or how cold it must be for them to wear such. Yet, for all the difference in apparent wealth, the atmosphere is genial. People joke and laugh and even wave to the knights and mages as they pass. Women and children can be seen washing their clothes, sewing, making candles, and various other things while every once in a while, the dragon spies a group of men working in lumber or a similar, heavier trade. Clearly, there's a lot to do in this medieval town, and somehow these people are happy to do it.

Still, as the knights travel upon the wide, cobblestone road, the buildings do begin to look nicer. Paint and stone bricks make an appearance as the buildings become a mix of businesses and large, middle class family dwellings. Flowers and vibrant gardens dot the street corners while the calls of merchants and busy folk color the air in rich overtones. It's all a bit overwhelming. The noises, the smells, the colors! It's all so bright to the little dragon, yet he can't bring himself to look away. He catches himself marveling at the difference in culture from what he's used to. Here, all the women wear long, colorful dresses and braid their hair in fine styles. The older women seem to favor keeping their hair up off of their necks in braided buns while the younger girls sport long braids down their backs. Each woman or girl wears a richly colored apron, and many sport bonnets. Their dresses seem to be either a two-piece ensemble with a vest, blouse, and skirt, or a dress with a button-up worn beneath a tank top style shoulder and chest area. Either way, the little dragon finds himself admiring the amount of work put into the dresses as he spies embroidered

Reborn as a Defective Drake: Snoweldon's Dragon

flowers or animals on almost every hem or cuff.

Meanwhile, the men all wear either breeches or, to his horror, tights. Sometimes in strange patterns or stripes. For their top half, most sport a solid colored, long sleeved tunic tucked into their breeches (or tights). On top of that, they wear a vest. Most of these vests are patterned with intricate embroidery or stringed tassel things that look like they belong in an antique store. Then again, everything the dragonet has seen so far has him thinking of a museum. Or a fairytale. Definitely a fairytale.

Surprisingly, an equal number of men seem to wear their hair long as there are men wearing their hair short. The more richly dressed or older men seem to prefer the longer styles, while many of the younger or lower class men wear their hair short. Perhaps long hair registered as a determination of wealth or status? At any rate, it all comes together to appear very historical European. Though the little dragon isn't certain of which part of historical Europe these folk resemble. He's not exactly a history buff after all.

Still, the little dragon's awe only grows as they pass a fountain with carved horses trotting around the centerpiece. The fountain sits in some sort of market square with buildings and vendors set up surrounding it. The lilting song of a flute and some sort of stringed instrument plays out over the busy economic center, while gaggles of children run about wildly. Rich tapestries coat the stalls here, and he can see several open air vendors with long lines around them. Picnic tables with large, cloth structures above them dot the area for families to eat at. As he watches, the little dragon can see some sort of service worker heading about the square lighting lanterns as the afternoon light casts long shadows through the marketplace. Truly, it feels as if he's been transported into some fantasy land, considering how bright and colorful everything and everyone is. Even as the knights trumble through and out of the area, the colorful lanterns and brightly colored fabrics remain a constant.

He's so engrossed in looking at the people and life of the city around him that he finds himself surprised to be passing through another portcullis. This portcullis doesn't have the

Reborn as a Defective Drake: Snoweldon's Dragon

added age or grime that the previous one had held. Instead, the light gray stone appears polished to the point of nearly being reflective. Darker specks of mottled gray dispute the illusion, but the little dragon can still see the clear care and work put into this wall. It's not exactly a surprising difference from the wall around the city, but it's still something distinct enough to register in the dragon's mind as different.

Life on the other side of the wall presents an even larger disparity between one wall and the next. Whereas the market and even the lower income areas were filled with the bustle and busy workers of a flourishing city, within this inner wall, the silence reigns almost eerily. Even as he takes it in, the dragonet has a hard time reconciling the clean, quiet, and empty courtyard inside the inner wall with the noisy environment he had just passed. The lengthening shadows of the evening don't grant the place any more life. Rather, the long shadows crawl across the earth like some strange creature of the night, ready to wake and create chaos.

Instead of cobblestone, heavy blocks of marble pave the path into the courtyard. A blue granite fountain trickles loudly in the center while its own centerpiece, a stone knight with a raised sword, stares forebodingly towards the entrance. Around the fountain, large fir trees stand in the place of the normal shrubbery. Their dark green needles reach the third floor of the structure behind the fountain, and the little dragon can only imagine how peaceful sitting at the base of one of

Reborn as a Defective Drake: Snoweldon's Dragon

them would be. Sadly, their impressive size blocks whatever lies behind them and he can only glimpse dark roof tiles and a few stone chimneys before the knights abruptly turn to the right.

Going along the wall, the group heads around to a smaller stone brick structure with a wide set of blue painted doors. Rich, red tapestries hang on either side with bright torches to light the way. A few finely dressed people linger outside the structure. One of them is holding the reins of a horse while a young lady sits upon the steed. The scent of hay and manure wafts out from what the little dragon assumes is a stable, albeit a nice one.

"Lady Lynn, greetings. Out for an evening ride?" Captain Snovalen called from the front of the group.

He dips his head in greeting but otherwise offers no bow of respect. Meanwhile, the brown-haired woman curtsies low before replying.

"Well met, Lord Snovalen. Yes, I am heading out for a ride shortly."

"Very well. Take care then." Lord Snovalen gives his farewell as he leads his group into the stables. Immediately the little dragon scrunches his nose in disgust. The air here reeks of horses and their manure much worse than the air outside. Multiple stalls line either wall down to the end of the stable, and torches light the dimness of the barn in flickering tongues of light.

Reborn as a Defective Drake: Snoweldon's Dragon

Immediately upon their entrance, teenage boys and girls come forward to take hold of the horses' reins. They are dressed similarly in red breeches, a white blouse, and open red vest with the exception of two slightly older looking boys who wear purple instead.

"Lord Snovalen, Lord Snoweldon has asked that you meet with him at the fifth bell." A blonde, red-clad girl steps forward as the captain dismounts. She holds several scrolls in her arms and stands somewhat rigidly like a soldier standing before a superior. "Lady Snovalen has also requested your presence for tea this afternoon and your grandson, Tyllwen, has returned from his trip to Willbeth. I believe he wishes to give you a gift he bought for you there since he missed your birthday. I also received a missive for you from Knight Eldwin's page and a note from High Mage Ern."

"I see. Please see to my horse and then report to the barracks for the evening meal and duties, Page Hillmet." Captain Snovalen replies as he takes the scrolls from the girl the dragon now knows is the captain's page. It's strange to see a girl as a page, but he just chalks it up to one of the good differences between this world and his old one. Behind him, he can hear the other pages approaching their knights and similar discussions being made. Oddly enough, he only hears one other person addressed as a page. The others are all addressed as 'Sirrah' instead.

Sadly, he doesn't have much time to think about it as

Page Hillmet begins taking off the bags on Captain Snovalen's horse. He hunkers down over the remaining meat in order to avoid being seen as she reaches to pull off the sack tied above his own. What's he to do? Hunker down and hope he doesn't get seen? Bolt for it? He's sure he can find food in the city and live there, so he's not too worried about leaving the rest of the meat chunk behind. Still, the rest of the knights haven't quite left the stables behind, and the mages are arguing with a page over something in one of their saddlebags. If he goes now and is caught will they kill him?

It's a frightening idea, one that sinks into his bones with frigid talons. Fear crawls along his spine as he plasters himself to the meat chunk. Squeezing his eyes shut, he struggles to remain still as the girl's hands close around the top of the sack and as she lifts it from the saddle. Suddenly, he finds himself shaking as the rough cloth bag swings back and forth.

"Eek!" The infant dragon can't help but squawk as his injured side brushes up against something. Bright pain burns up his side at the rough texture of the rucksack, and he wiggles away from the side. Abruptly, the movement stops. Heart pounding, he struggles to remain still and quiet.

"Oi, Hillmet, what's wrong?" a young male voice calls from somewhere behind the dragonet.

Again, the sack cloth moves, and he thinks that maybe the page girl is gesturing at him.

"This bag just squeaked, and I think I saw it move. I'm

Reborn as a Defective Drake: Snoweldon's Dragon

simply wondering if a mouse might have gotten inside at some point." Hillmet explains haughtily. She huffs, and the bag moves again, so the dragonet surmises that she's holding it at arms' length.

"Oh what? Is the big bad city lady scared of a little rodent?" the male asks tauntingly.

"No!"

The sharp retort and consequent shifting of the rucksack drags the little dragon's wing and side against the fabric again, but this time he hunkers down to suffer quietly. Tears burden his eyes, but no sound escapes his snout at the rough handling.

"I'm not afraid of some stupid mouse! Maybe you're the one afraid of a mouse, Koptur," Hillmet squawked angrily.

She waved the bag around again, and this time the little dragon can't help but let out a high pitched whimper as his injured side is rubbed against the sack repeatedly.

Once more, the children fall silent while the dragonet cringes. Shoot. They definitely heard him now. Slowly, the bag is laid upon a flat surface. He assumes it's the stable floors due to the feeling of slight weightlessness going downwards. The fabric rustles, and he squeezes his eyes even tighter as a shadow falls over him. For a moment, nothing moves. It's as if a spell has been cast over the world and has frozen it into timeless purity. Then the infantile dragon blinks his eyes open to look up at two shocked children staring down at him. A pair

Reborn as a Defective Drake: Snoweldon's Dragon

of onyx and a pair of ruby eyes widen in shock.

The little dragon squeaks in nervous surprise.

The girl shrieks and leaps back.

The boy's eyes roll back into his head and he topples.

And... he decides that it is most certainly time to get out of here.

Reborn as a Defective Drake: Snoweldon's Dragon

Even though his right shoulder burns, he knows he needs to disappear. Every breath comes as a panicked gasp that doesn't do much for him as he runs as quickly as his tiny, infantile body will allow towards the stable entrance. Behind him, the remaining conscious page shrieks something unintelligent, and the blue clothed ones scatter with sharp cries of shock. Sadly, the knights are still in the building even if their captain has long left for his own pursuits.

"What the-"

The dragon runs under a person he believes is the woman knight due to the high-pitched shriek she lets out at his passing. He's about the size of a mouse, but surely a knight wouldn't be scared of a mouse? Still, he does seem to have the advantage of surprise over the knights as they instinctively move back from his swift form.

"By the great Lady!" Sir Camuel cries as he hobbles back from the little dragon in shock.

In response, the infant dragon merely darts under his raised foot. Sadly, not all of these knights appear to be complete greenhorns.

Reborn as a Defective Drake: Snoweldon's Dragon

"It's a monster! It must have fallen through the rift and ridden back with us!" The golden-haired knight shouts as he moves forward.

Behind him, the quiet knight follows his lead with a frown of his lips.

"Get it quick!" The golden-haired knight unsheathes his sword and steps between the little dragon and the stable entrance.

"Eeep!" The dragon lets out a shriek and skitters to a halt before the blonde knight. The man towers over the little dragon, and as he raises his sword, the little dragon feels fear stiffen his spine. He jumps away more from instinct than with any rational thought and can feel the displacement of air on his snout as he catapults himself backwards. The silver of the sword gleams mere inches before him. Gulping, he doesn't wait for the man to raise his sword and try again. Instead, his eyes dart wildly for a place to hide.

There! A pile of hay, likely meant for the horses' bedding, sits against one of the stone walls. With his small size, finding him inside of the pile would be like finding a needle in a haystack! Well, maybe. He is a bit bigger than a needle, but he's still confident in his ability to evade capture!

The little dragon bolts toward the hay so quickly his claws skid across the cobblestone foundation for a moment before finding traction. Behind him, another sharp song of quickly moving air tells him of the danger remaining still

Reborn as a Defective Drake: Snoweldon's Dragon

would bring. Then, he's diving into the hay and squirming his way through prickly dried grass stalks. Steel skims across the side of his tail with fearsome speed before he manages to worm his way deeper into the haystack. The sharp scent of blood mixes into the scent of dried hay while the end of his tail burns painfully.

Ughhh! He thinks to himself at the cloying stench of hay.

As a human, he actually enjoyed the smell. As a dragon, it's definitely an overpoweringly sweet smell when shrouded in its midst. The smell and the sensation of the dried stalks on his scales make for a distinctly uncomfortable hiding place. Sadly, it's also a very temporary hiding place.

"Don't let it get away! Dig through and find it!" the blonde knight orders.

The little dragon can hear the sound of armored hands clinking together as the knights begin sifting through the hay. Above him, the pressure of the air changes, and he rolls over just in time to avoid a grasping hand. He scrambles toward the back of the haystack where it meets the wall. Behind the little dragon, light has begun to filter through the dried grass from the knights' searching. From what he can tell, the two men are scooping up handfuls of hay at a time before checking and then chunking it when he's not in it. Turning, the dragon presses his back and wings against the stone wall to put as much distance between him and the knights as he can.

Maybe they'll give up soon?

Reborn as a Defective Drake: Snoweldon's Dragon

"Where is it? I don't see it." The woman hisses.

Apparently, she'd gotten over her fear and also joined in the search at some point.

"It's in here somewhere, just keep digging!" the blonde knight commands.

The light coming from the front of the haystack becomes brighter to the left, and the dragon gives a quiet whine in response. He shuffles slightly to the right, still pressed up against the wall, and squeaks when he tumbles backwards. Blinking, he stares upwards at the red-streaked evening sky. From inside the stable, he can still hear the noises of the knights as they shift through the haystack in search of him. Tilting his head, the little dragon just stares at the mouse hole he had accidentally tumbled through. Or actually, it looked like it was meant to be there, so maybe some sort of water drain? For when the stable floors were cleaned or if a bucket was spilled perhaps?

Either way, he's not going to be sticking around. Soon, the knights will realize he's not there and either see the drainage hole or expand their search radius. Rolling over, the little dragon hisses in pain before forcing himself to his legs. His shoulder still hurts, the raw spots on his wings were irritated by the hay, and his tail is still leaking blood everywhere. He's covered in black ash from the lava field, blood from his wounds, and dirt from rolling around everywhere. He feels and looks disgusting. It's beyond time to

Reborn as a Defective Drake: Snoweldon's Dragon

get somewhere safe and take a bath, maybe drink some water too since his throat feels so dry.

Looking around, he charts his course towards the area behind the huge, U-shaped castle the group of knights had passed. People live here, so there must be either a well or somewhere with good water access. If he didn't find a well or something, then he could at least find where the residents here did the laundry and go from there. Limping, he skulks around the barn since some large bushes and grasses grow alongside the building's exterior.

Sadly, most of the interior of the fortress's compound is composed of neatly tended grass, some hedges and bushes, a few flower beds, and large pine trees. The grass is so short that the dragon's not sure if he'll have an easier time of it bolting across the grass or using his light coloring as camouflage on the cobblestone pathways. Still, he really can't afford to stay near the barn now that the knights have seen him. Luckily, there don't seem to be too many people in this section of the compound. Rather, there seems to be a riding paddock, a paddock filled with grass and a few mares, the stable behind him, and a few other structures that he would assume could be related to horses. The area's also on the far side of the compound, so while he can see the castle from here, it's not particularly close to where the dragonet would assume most of the hustle and bustle is. Most likely, this is to prevent the castle's inhabitants from being bothered by the smell of horse

Reborn as a Defective Drake: Snoweldon's Dragon

manure or the sound of barn animals.

However, being so far from the castle and presumably the rest of the fortress's work areas fits the little dragon's agenda just fine. Most of the pages and knights were occupied towards the front of the building since they only needed to tend to the horses' tack or see to their assigned duties. Behind the stable, only stable hands or people with jobs related specifically to horses linger. In other words, it's absolutely deserted with the horses having already been fed and tended to earlier in the day.

He can see one stable hand giving a horse a brush down, but beyond that, this area isn't occupied. Taking a deep breath, the infant dragon limps forward as quickly as he can make himself without imminent threat to his life. He makes it to a rose bush and looks around carefully. He doesn't see anyone, but the sound of clopping hooves causes him to duck under the bush's thorny arms. Peering out, he spies a horse-drawn cart entering from a side gate. A few barrels and rucksacks ride along in the back of the cart. This must be how the castle gets its food and supplies, the little dragon realizes. He glances between the cart coming his way and the gate he hadn't noticed. Instead of being an iron-barred, heavy, lifting gate, the side gate is merely two heavy oak doors that swing on ancient hinges.

Clearly, no one was worried about this gate making an impression on people. Two guards can be seen outside the gate before it closes, but none oversee the area immediately inside. This bodes well for the dragon, as two alert guards facing the interior would make slipping by infinitely more difficult, even in the deepening twilight. He can't help but wonder if security is always so lax though. Surely a castle would have more security? Maybe they're underfunded?

Shrugging, the dragon watches the horse-drawn carriage pass him by. Behind him, the driver slows to a stop and starts up a conversation with the stablehand.

"Busy today?" the old man on the wagon calls out.

"No more than every day. How do you fare today?" the boy asks.

The dragon can hear the grin in the boy's voice. The boy must know the cart driver pretty well. Still, a distraction is a distraction. Taking advantage of the two's conversation, the little dragon darts from his place underneath a rose bush to the tall grass growing around and in the mare's pasture. He's small enough that he can easily hide within the lush stalks. Peering back, he sees that the dark-haired stable hand and the old cart driver have remained oblivious to his progress across the grounds.

"Now, watch out for firebugs, you hear? The little fiends like to cause trouble in the summer. If they get into the hay, 'tis a right nightmare. 'Specially if one of the horses eats it by mistake. Now that's a mess to clean up once it comes out the other end," the old man warns the boy.

Reborn as a Defective Drake: Snoweldon's Dragon

"I'll watch out, Farmer Enthrik. Thank you for your wisdom." The boy smiles here. "However, if you're late again, Head Cook Minnam might give you a scolding again. You know she likes punctuality. You're carrying the vegetables for the lord's dinner, aren't you?"

"By the snowy peaks of the Weldwitts, you're right, Little Fin. 'Tis time I got on. Be good now, you hear?" The old man whips his reins to send the horse walking forward.

The dragonet takes this chance to scurry further towards the other end of the grass pasture. Peaking out, he can see the dirt pasture in the corner of the fortress, likely for training or exercising the horses, and an ivy covered stone brick wall separating the equestrian area from whatever area lay around the curve of the main castle building. It has a small portcullis draped over with ivy.

Nodding to himself, the little dragon looks around for anyone watching before hurrying over to the cobblestone wall. Once there, he peaks back to make sure he wasn't seen, but doesn't see anyone but the stable hand who has begun leading the horse back towards the stable. He breathes a sigh of relief. No knights, no spell casters, and no humans. He's doing all right so far. The dragon limps over to the opening in the cobblestone wall, only to find himself staring up at a heavy oaken door. With the shadows cast by the setting sun, he hadn't been able to see the door through the overhanging ivy. Now he finds himself facing a conundrum. He can't open the

Reborn as a Defective Drake: Snoweldon's Dragon

door, being so small, and the wall is far too steep to climb. To make matters worse, he can hear the trickling of water from just behind the wall. It almost feels as if the water is taunting him, being just out of reach.

Letting out a whine, the dragon lets his head fall forward onto the door with a soft thud. He's so close, it's as if he can taste it! Is he just supposed to wait until someone comes over and goes through the door?

Growling to himself, he lifts his head and gives another heavy hit to the door. His temper beats like a drum in his head and his heart, and frustration mounts within him. It's not fair! He's been kicked out of the nest by his siblings, almost eaten by weird snowy ice monsters, been scared out of his life by a giant monster chicken, swallowed by fake water, dumped randomly near some knights with monster-killing issues, and been chased by said knights even though he had done absolutely nothing to them!

He releases out a high pitched whine and raises his uninjured shoulder to scratch loudly at the door. He wants water, dang it! Tilting his head up, he lets a mix between a yelp and rumbly growl leave his snout.

It's not fair to be so close and not get water!

Whining, he thumps the door with his head and doesn't care at the pain that laces across his skull at the action. He's about to give another long, loud scratch to the door when he hears movement on the other side.

Reborn as a Defective Drake: Snoweldon's Dragon

"Bertholdt, did you get locked out again?" A sweet, high-pitched child's voice calls from the other side. The dragon's eyes widen as he hears someone lift a latch and turn the door handle. He leans back in shock, rearing up on his hind legs with his front paws in the air as if to beg. The door opens, and the little dragon is left staring at what must be the most adorable child he has even seen.

She's probably somewhere between five and eight with curly, blonde hair framing her face in a myriad of braids and long, healthy locks. The setting sun behind her lights the edges of her hair into brilliant shades of orange and red. He can't tell what color her eyes are, but from what he can see of her shadowed face, the girl has cherubic, delicate features and a tiny button nose. She's dressed similarly to the women from the town, but her clothes feature a wealth several cuts above the rest. Fine embroidery lingers on every hem; from the dark blue of her skirt and vest to the startling red of her apron. Though, on her, the apron appears less an apron and more a dynamic layer of cloth that happens to be shaped like an apron. It's certainly not meant to be dirtied in the kitchen with all of the careful embroidering and the sheer, shimmering sash tying it in place.

She's undeniably adorable with her still-there baby fat and wide eyes. However, the little dragon is sure he'd feel much better if those eyes weren't pinned on him.

Reborn as a Defective Drake: Snoweldon's Dragon

Reborn as a Defective Drake: Snoweldon's Dragon

The Princess (not really) and the Dragon (sort of)

With a squeak, the dragon finds himself leaning back and toppling flat on his back. It doesn't feel great, considering parts of his wings have been rubbed raw. Blinking, he freezes at the sensation of chubby fingers curling under his wings and back. Above him, shadowed eyes and blonde hair loom too close for comfort. Terror wells up under the muscles of his throat, and he can't help but produce a high-pitched sound as he unsuccessfully tries to wiggle away. Instead, her fingers lift him into the air with a distinctly stomach-wrenching quality, and he finds himself face-to-face and eye-to-eye with the young girl.

"Mrrp," Is the only thing he can manage as she appraises him.

Her hands move again, and he tenses in preparation for something bad to happen. Only, with lips pursed in concentration, she gently rolls him onto his stomach and draws her eyebrows together in displeasure.

"You're hurt," she murmurs childishly.

Her nose wrinkles.

"And dirty," she declares before she's moving back through the portcullis with the little dragon cradled safely in her hands.

Her statement certainly rings true. The baby dragon is covered in dirt, ash, and blood from the last forty-eight hours. However, any embarrassment he might have felt is washed away as the dragon is carried through the stone doorway. Instead, the little dragon looks around in awe from the center of the girl's cupped hands.

Calling the area a garden would have technically been true, but only true in the same sense someone could say that a lion is a cat or that the Marriana trench is deep. The world beyond the garden gate is a world wholly different from the equine-focused areas behind him. Ivy covers the walls in shimmering shades of sunset touched green. The path below leads the way with shimmering multi-colored stones, bordered by obsidian pave stones and a tall, healthy hedge. Moss edges up on the paved stones in green assurances of peaceful times. Between the hedge and the paved stones, long stemmed blossoms of the purple and white variants sway in an evening breeze. After a few yards, the hedge opens up to reveal a blue marble fountain with a wide circular basin and a rearing horse situated at the center. Water pours from the horse's mouth in a way that the little dragon finds somewhat funny, since it looks like the horse is spitting water out to fill the basin.

Reborn as a Defective Drake: Snoweldon's Dragon

The colored cobblestones create a circular patio area around the basin. Some red porcelain planters hold herbs or flowers, and a long stone table with benches sits on the side of the fountain closest to the castle. Behind the fountain, attached to the outer wall of the fortress, a carved horse spews water from its mouth down into a pond that stretches along the exterior of the garden. In the evening light it's difficult to tell, but the little dragon thinks he can see something glowing from within the depths of it, shining up around the lily pads, frogs, and flowers that inhabit the surface of the pond. Tall firs and pines ring the fountain's cobbled courtyard, and ferns coat their undersides with leafy hideaways.

Glass and metal trinkets hang from the trees in glimmering specs of light as they catch the last lights of the sun. A few stone benches have been placed around the courtyard, and he can see another wall of hedge rising on the other side to border another colorful path out of the garden. Towards the castle, a set of stairs rises into a large, column-encased area: a pavilion crafted using only the finest marble. Ivy crawls on the columns, and he can see a few people milling about in the lantern light there. The garden is empty save for the dragon and the girl, however.

The child approaches the fountain and gently, or at least, far more gently than the dragon would expect from a little girl, places him on the fountain's outer stone ring. Blinking, the little dragon turns his attention back to the little

Reborn as a Defective Drake: Snoweldon's Dragon

girl just in time for him to see her pull an embroidered pouch from its place at her waist.

"Here you go," the girl mumbles as she extracts an embroidered handkerchief from the pouch.

She dips it into the clear water, and the dragon finds himself starting once the water stills and he can see his reflection on the water's surface. He looks awful, and the sight is enough to bring heat to his cheeks. Dried blood flecks his muzzle while his right side and neck appear almost painted with it. Deep red teeth marks show where he was bitten on his neck while three long claw marks mar the flesh of his shoulder. Their coloring reminds him of the deep red of the interior of a cherry pie, but the unease the sight strikes to his heart is very real.

The wounds have scabbed over, but only in the sense that the blood has become too congealed along the surface of the wound. The swelling and discoloration along the right side of his body attests to the depth of damage the icy serpent's claws had inflicted upon him. His front makes a gruesome sight. Meanwhile, his underbelly and legs are coated in mud. Instead of the pearlescent white of his scales, his legs look more similar to sticks or tiny tree trunks with their muddy shades of brown and clumpy surface texture. His wings and back remain coated in the dull gray ash of the lava region he had glided over with lighter streaks where the frost of the snowy mountain region had worn away some of the ash. As a

Reborn as a Defective Drake: Snoweldon's Dragon

whole, he's literally covered in some of the worst filth, and he certainly has no place in a clean, almost mystical environment like this girl's garden.

To his surprise, actual color rushes over his scaly face to add a tint of blush just below his eyes at the thought.

Huh, dragons could blush. Who knew?

He squeaks a bit as frigid water touches his back. Jolting, he throws his head back with wide eyes to catch the little girl in the process of dabbing at his back with her wet handkerchief.

"Shh, shh," the girl coos. "It's okay."

Again, she dabs at his back with her wet cloth, and he forces himself not to hiss in displeasure of it. The cold temperature of the cloth almost burns at his scales, but she appears to be washing him, and he really wants to be clean. She rinses the embroidered fabric, and he winces at the filth. Will the clearly expensive handkerchief ever be the same?

Then she works her attentions higher, towards his shoulder, and he shrieks at the sharp burst of pain her actions elicit. Striking instinct and inappropriate desperation overtake his rational brain, and he reacts without conscious thought. Rolling, he manuervers himself away from her and takes a snap at her hands in warning. A sharp, high pitched hiss emanates from his throat like some sort of angry cat. Eyes widening, the girl whips her hands away and falters. He bares his teeth at her and growls lowly. He can feel that his breath has sped up, and

Reborn as a Defective Drake: Snoweldon's Dragon

the thumping of his heart pounds loudly within his skull. A moment goes by, and he finds himself blinking as the haze of instinct begins to wear thin over his mind.

"Hey." The quiet murmur pulls at his attention, and he finds himself staring into wary blue eyes. "It's okay. Calm down," the girl soothes as she puts both hands in front of her slowly. "I didn't mean to, I'm sorry," she soothes when he straightens slowly. "Shh, shh." Her calm voice brings him back fully from the haze the pain had brought, and he finds himself calming. His heart slows, and his breath eases. He allows himself to relax as she approaches again.

"That's where you're hurt, right?" She brushes her fingers in a wide circle around the ragged claw marks to his shoulder and the bite to his neck. "I'm sorry, I'll be more careful. But I need to clean your wound so it won't be infected. If it gets infected, it'll hurt even more than it does now."

She moves to continue dabbing at him, but he finds himself moving away with a grumpy growl. He doesn't want to be in any more pain. He knows on a rational level that what the girl says is true; he does need to clean his wounds, especially the bite. Who knows what kind of bacteria was growing in that ice snake's mouth?

But another part, the bit of him that he's slowly coming to see as the baby dragon part of him, doesn't want to allow her to touch him somewhere so vulnerable and painful. He doesn't want her to see his weakness, and he doesn't want her to cause

Reborn as a Defective Drake: Snoweldon's Dragon

him pain. All of that combined leaves him making rumbly whines from the back of his throat in upset.

The girl frowns. It's obvious that she thinks he's being silly, but she doesn't quite want to risk his sharp baby teeth or claws to continue. She narrows her eyes at him. He gives her a glare in return. For a moment, their stare-off continues. Then she looks heavenward, closes her eyes, gives a huff of a sigh, and looks back at him in irritated resignment.

"Well, I suppose this only leaves one solution," she declares.

The little dragon relaxes, thinking he has won. He has not. He has merely fallen into complacency that doesn't help him at all when she shoves him into the fountain. Putting one hand under her apron to protect her from any claws or teeth, the little girl sweeps him into the fountain pitilessly.

"Eeek!" He shrieks as he hits the water. The shock of it freezes him in place before he gives another shriek and begins panicking. Clawing at the water, the little dragon manages to break the surface and cough. Before he can even gain his bearing, small, evil hands scoop him out of the water and back onto the outer rim of the fountain. Immediately, he hunches over himself and begins shivering. Despite the last of the day's sunlight still being present, there's not much warmth left in it, and the breeze leaves him absolutely freezing.

"There you go. Now all the blood and dirt's been washed away." The girl smiles at him, but he can't help but cringe.

Reborn as a Defective Drake: Snoweldon's Dragon

Goodness, whatever happened to that kind soothing voice she had been using before? He liked that voice better!

"Hmmm..." she murmurs as she looks over him speculatively. She furrows her blond brows and purses her dainty lips while she rests her hands on her hips. "I thought you were just a lost min-wyv, but you're not, are you? You have front legs. And you're white. I've never seen a white min-wyv." He sneezes and hunkers lower while she speaks. He doesn't know what a min-wyv is, but he's starting to lose feeling in his wing-tips and paws.

A lizard that walks on two legs? Who's ever heard of that?

"Achoo!" He sneezes again.

That finally gets the girl's attention.

"Oh, right. I need to dry you off, don't I? You have scales, so you're probably a reptile, and even magic reptiles get cold when they run out of magic," she babbles.

Reaching out, she scoops him up before sitting on a dry portion of the fountain rim. Once done, she sets him in her lap and flops the edges over him. He's left to balk for all of a moment before gentle touches begin massaging the cloth along his back. She's careful not to reach his shoulders or neck. After a moment, she teases her fingers under his stomach and begins drying him there.

Unable to stop himself, the little dragon lets out a croon at the feeling of the cloth rubbing along the sensitive scales of his underbelly. Is this what dogs feel when you rub their belly?

Reborn as a Defective Drake: Snoweldon's Dragon

If so, he can understand why they like it so much! He practically melts in her lap as his wings sag and his head droops in bliss.

"Oh, you like having your belly rubbed!" The girl exclaims in joy from above him.

If he had the muscle control to nod, he would, but as it is, he simply croons louder and relaxes further into her hands. This continues for several moments before she uncovers him from her apron. Blinking, he looks up at her. The last drops of sunlight have faded from the garden now, and her shadowed face seems dormant of the care she had exuded before. In the lantern light, half of her face gleams in golden hues of implacable seriousness while the other half remains a dark abyss.

"Still... what exactly are you?" she murmurs quietly, almost more to herself than to him.

"You're definitely not a min-wyv, and I've never heard of a normal lizard with wings before..." The girl peers at him for a few moments more before someone's sharp call breaks her concentration.

"Lady Cecily!" a woman's voice calls from the pavilion atop the stairs.

A lone figure waits there in the lantern light, the others having dispersed at some point. From this distance, the little dragon can make out a white bonnet and a blue dress.

"Lady Cecily, 'tis time for supper." The woman calls

Reborn as a Defective Drake: Snoweldon's Dragon

again.

The blond girl above him gasps and looks back down at him. Nodding to herself, Cecily, for that must be her name, wraps him in her wet handkerchief and shoves him unceremoniously into her cloth pouch. The little dragon barely has enough time to squeak a protest before Cecily's shushing him and tying the bag back to the sash around her waist. Muted darkness awaits him in the confines of her bag. The wet handkerchief rests uncomfortably moist against his body as well.

"Hush," she murmurs. "If mother finds out I picked you up, she'll make me throw you out."

Blinking, the little dragon wonders if she can tell he understands her or if she just talks to animals like that all the time. Either way, the drawstrings of the pouch are drawn shut by her nimble fingers, and he finds himself trapped in the darkness of the purse. He doesn't particularly want to be found by someone more inclined to murder infant dragons than Cecily, so he resigns himself to silence. He feels movement as she begins walking and answers the woman calling her.

"Coming, Alya. I was just admiring the sunset," Cecily answers the woman's calls as she begins climbing the steps to the pavilion.

The little dragon can feel as her gait levels out and listens as the girl begins conversing with Alya on the way to what he supposes must be supper. He hopes nothing bad will

Reborn as a Defective Drake: Snoweldon's Dragon

come of this, but as Cecily carries him away from the gardens, a pit of nerves settles into his stomach.

For a few moments, all the dragon hears is the clip-clap of wooden soles on cobblestone pathways. From inside Cecily's purse, the dragonet only perceives a slight lightening as she approaches a torch before darkness swallows him again as she passes by it. Then, the ominous creak of an old door accompanies a distinct lightening of the cloth around him as Cecily enters what he assumes to be the castle. He wiggles slightly at the echo from her wooden shoes on the stone floors. Wherever they are, it's very big to have such wide and distant-sounding echoes.

Pressure curves its way around him, and he realizes that Cecily has cupped a hand around her bag at his movement, likely to keep him still and avoid detection. Huffing, he curls up slightly in the pouch, hoping to present a more normal-looking purse to anyone looking. Honestly, if she just hadn't grabbed him and stuffed him in her bag, she could have avoided this whole experience.

Rolling his eyes, the little dragon listens as the sharp sounds of Cecily's shoes fade into a muffled shuffling sound. She must have hit some sort of carpet or rug. Ahead, he can hear the sharp clangs of metal and stone greeting one another. Low voices also trickle into his ears. In another few of Cecily's steps, the little dragon can make out distinct voices.

"I do believe this harvest is going to be a good one, Father," a deep, male voice murmurs.

"That's good. The frost came too early for most of our greens last year. We were only able to harvest the tubers," an older, cracked voice responds.

"If I have to eat turnips for a week straight again, I'm going on a diet," a young--but older than Cecily--boy announced. Several hearty chuckles, and a few giggles sounded out.

"Don't be so mean to your vegetables, Connor. They might start an uprising against you." Another male voice, this one sounding to belong to a young adult or older teen comments mirthfully..

"Don't be so mean to your younger siblings, Calvin; they might start an uprising against you," the boy, Connor, snarks back.

"Boys," a woman interrupts ominously. "None of that at the table. Connor, put your spoon down. It is not a catapult, and your food is not your ammunition. Calvin, stop teasing your little brother. You didn't like your vegetables either at that age." Despite the curt edge the woman's tone held at the beginning of her chastisement, by the end of it the frigid tone had given way to warm affection.

Reborn as a Defective Drake: Snoweldon's Dragon

The clank of a spoon meeting a ceramic bowl follows her statement, so the little dragon assumes the woman's words have been followed. Is she perhaps the boys' and Cecily's mother?

"Cecily, you're late again," the first voice, the deep male voice speaks up again, and the little dragon feels Cecily's steps falter for a moment.

"Yes, Father. Apologies. I found something interesting in the garden," Cecily answers demurely.

Her tone contrasts sharply with the bright, inquisitive gaze the little dragon had been subjected to in the garden. The likely reason why becomes apparent in the next moment as the woman speaks up again.

"Cecily, you've dirtied your dress and apron again," the woman reprimands sharply.

The little dragon feels Cecily flinch even as the girl slides into a seat.

"Yes, Mother. Apologies," Cecily says quietly.

The little dragon picks up the sound of a harsh gust of air.

"When will you cease your childish behavior? You're eight now, Cecily. It's time you started acting more like a young lady. You're not a babe to wander around and get into trouble anymore," the woman, Cecily's mother, continues.

Beneath him, the little dragon can feel Cecily grow tense and strained.

Reborn as a Defective Drake: Snoweldon's Dragon

Poor child, he thinks to himself.

He still remembers that odd period between toddlerhood and preteen when his own mother had first started imposing rules to go along with his age. It hadn't been a pleasant learning curve. If only his mother had told him "no" as a toddler instead of letting him grow up to be a little rascal of a child, he might have had a better time of it.

"Oh, come now, Selina. There's still time before she has to take up any duties or familial training. She can have a bit more fun before then. She's only going to be young once," Cecily's father intervenes.

There's a moment of tension before he can hear another sigh as Selina gives way to her husband's appeasement.

"Very well, Conwell, but she won't stay little for long. Eventually, she will need to behave with the dignity and conduct befitting of a lady of her standing. She is your only daughter. There are expectations that come with that."

The little dragon scrunches his nose at the woman's dark undertone.

Ouch. That's kind of hurtful.

He feels the bitter taste of disappointment sneak up his throat. With all of the female knights and pages, he had been hopeful that women were given more thought than their medieval surroundings might suggest.

"There may be expectations, but that doesn't mean we are beholden to them. We are the Snoweldons. We hold ice in our lungs and the frigid waters of the Nix Fons in our veins. Our people reflect that, be they man or woman. Cecily isn't a woman of the plains. She's Snoweldon through and through," Conwell, Cecily's father, speaks aggressively.

Beneath him, Cecily shifts uncomfortably, and the little dragon realizes that this isn't something new to her. The current topic had likely been thrown around the table more than a few times.

"Conwell--" Selina begins.

"Selina," Conwell interrupts. "I will not treat my daughter as anything less than she is simply because you are uncomfortable at the idea that a daughter you've raised won't be as prim and proper as your family. She won't be marrying a plains man, so her decorum towards herself and others won't be an issue."

The man's words rest heavy and forbidding in the air, but the little dragon finds himself sitting up in interest. So there was a Snoweldon area, likely very cold and snowy, and there was a plains area. And both of them have differing cultures, at least so much as to have different views on people and what rights they were entitled to. Were the plains part of a neighboring country, or the same? If they were part of a foriegn power, the plains would have likely been referred to by name. Also, if he's reading the conversation correctly, it would mean that the mother, Selina, was foriegn, and she had neither the accent nor the difference in features that he would expect in a

Reborn as a Defective Drake: Snoweldon's Dragon

foreigner. So most likely, Selina was from a different region. Apparently, an area defined by plains.

"As you wish," Selina murmurs after a moment of silence.

From her tone, the little dragon knows that she's not happy with Conwell's decision, but that she's not pursuing the argument for now. Beneath him, Cecily finally relaxes her muscles, and he can hear a slight sigh of relief from above him. Around the table, the sounds of cutlery against pottery makes an uneasy appearance. After that uncomfortable conversation, it seems that the family can begin eating.

"So, how was your first horsemanship class, Connor?" the elder brother, Calvin asks.

"It was fun! Sir Gerran says I have to start slow at first, so I've been riding an old mare named Patience. She's kind of slow, but if you put a carrot in front of her, she'll trot and canter for you. Sir Gerran says not to do it too much, or she'll get fat, though." Connor gleefully expounds upon his day.

He sounds so childishly infatuated with his lessons and the old mare that the little dragon can't help but allow a pleased rumble to escape.

Ah, children. So bright and optimistic.

Immediately, he feels Cecily's free hand wrap around her purse in warning.

"Cecily, are you feeling well?" Conwell asks from where the dragon assumes the head of the table is. Cecily shifts uncomfortably at her father's question, and her voice is distinctly embarrassed when she replies.

"Yes, father. My stomach is just a little upset today. That's all." Again, her hand squeezes around his scales in warning.

Thankfully, the pressure isn't much. The girl seems to know she can't just squeeze him willy nilly without hurting him, and he's grateful for it.

"I see... Do you need to see a healer then? Or maybe have some medicine?" Cecily's father asks.

The little dragon can practically taste the honey pouring from his tongue. Goodness, but he must spoil his only daughter! The little dragon doubts the man would be half so sickly sweet to his sons.

"No, I'm fine. It's mostly just noisy," Cecily squeaks out in embarrassment.

"All right, then. If anything changes, make sure to report to one of the healers. There's been an illness going around in town."

The dragon's head perks slightly at Conwell's concern.

An illness? That's not good. Medieval societies don't have good medical care, so illnesses that wouldn't normally be too bad can spread and kill like wildfire.

"Yes, Father," Cecily concedes dutifully.

"The same goes for both of you: Connor, Calvin. If either of you feels ill, visit the healers' hall for a check up. I don't want

Reborn as a Defective Drake: Snoweldon's Dragon

anyone in our family falling sick," Selina pipes up strictly.

"Yes, mother," The boys reply in tandem.

Despite a good few years separating them in age, their synchronicity spoke of a healthy brotherhood. And perhaps a bit of mischief if the longsuffering in their voices was any indication. The dragon bites down a warble of amusement but can't help the smile that spreads across his face.

Jeez, how did such a strict lady get such bright and happy children? Definitely the dad's doing. Or were the children raised by nursemaids in this medieval society?

The little dragon isn't sure what time period this society adheres the most to or even if he can base his understanding of this world's culture on Earth's medieval societies.

Cecily sets her cutlery down with a soft pat.

"Father," The little girl enquires primly. "May I please be excused? I've finished eating."

"Are you sure, Cecily? You've hardly touched your sweet potatoes, and those are your favorite." Conwell's voice carries concern, and the little dragon practically feels the scrutiny Cecily must be under right now.

"Yes, Father. I'm just not very hungry tonight. I must have drunk too much tea this afternoon with Mother. Apologies." Cecily tenses under the little dragon's claws.

"Cecily," Selaine murmurs in reproach. "I told you that you were drinking too much tea."

"Yes, Mother. I'm very sorry. I'll drink more water next

Reborn as a Defective Drake: Snoweldon's Dragon

time when dance practice has made me thirsty."

"See that you do, Cecily. It's unbecoming to be unable to eat the food someone else has provided for you."

"Well, if you're sure it's nothing more than that, you may retire early tonight." Cacily's father assents to his daughter's request gracefully. "Sleep well, my child."

"Yes, Father. You, as well. Good night Mother, Grandfather, Calvin, Connor." Cecily bids her family goodnight before she stands, one hand on her waist pouch keeping the dragonet still.

Her family's replies echo across the stone behind them as she swiftly makes her exit. Two heeled feet follow her, and the little dragon wonders if it's the woman from earlier that escorted her to dinner.

"Lady Cecily, I have a tonic for your stomach. I'm sure it will help you feel better."

Ahah! It is the woman who escorted Cecily into dinner. Is she perhaps the girl's minder or personal attendant? Wasn't her name A-something? Anna maybe?

"Thank you, Alya, but I think I'll be just fine. I'm sure it's just from drinking too much at tea time," Cecily assures the woman without slowing her pace.

Her gait changes, and the dragon feels his stomach drop a bit as the girl begins climbing a set of stairs. He does his best to make a layout of the castle, but all he really knows is that he's being carried to the second floor. Or maybe the third? It

Reborn as a Defective Drake: Snoweldon's Dragon

seems as if the girl has entered a winding staircase, as he's certain she's been climbing too long to have only risen one floor. Still, eventually her movements even out. He stops feeling the change in height, so he assumes they must have reached the right floor.

Again, Cecily's footsteps change as her wooden clogs hit some sort of rug or carpet. This must be an important area to have a carpet. After a few more paces, Cecily comes to a halt and addresses Alya.

"Alya, I don't require your assistance tonight. You may leave for the evening."

"But Milady," Alya murmurs. "Your bath--"

"I just bathed yesterday, Alya. It'll be okay if I sponge off quickly in the morning before my lessons. I'll take a proper soak tomorrow afternoon before my mother calls me for tea time."

"... Very Well, Milady, if you insist," Alya reluctantly agrees, and the little dragon can hear the sound of her feet shuffling away.

A moment later, the woman's own clogs shuffle along the carpet and fade into the distance. The little dragon picks up the faint clack as she reaches the end of the carpeted area and begins her descent down the staircase. Pressed up against her side, Cecily's exaggerated sigh of relief swings the pouch he's in like an unexpected tire-swing ride.

"Squearrk!" he yelps.

Reborn as a Defective Drake: Snoweldon's Dragon

Immediately, Cecily's hands curl tightly around the pouch, and she swerves around dizzyingly. The little dragon finds himself thrown onto his back as the sound of a heavy door being thrown open and closed crashes above his head. Cecily's footsteps thump across another carpeted area before she's grabbing the pouch from her waist and setting it on something soft. Light pours in above him as she opens the pouch. He blinks dazedly before gentle hands pull him up and set him on soft fabric.

"Now, what was all that about at dinner, huh? It's not like you can understand me. Little monsters like you aren't that smart," Cecily bites out.

The little dragon looks up and notes her crossed arms and angry demeanor. She's glaring at him like he ate the last piece of cake with one leg propped in a semi-dramatic pose.

I can too understand you. You just can't understand me, he chirps grumpily.

He makes sure not to bare his teeth, but he gives her the best angry stare he can manage. With a snout and no true eyebrows, he's not sure how well he manages it, but he hopes he conveys his full irritation to the child. No one likes being picked up and randomly shoved in bags and carried around like a potato. Honestly, if he were a real wild animal, she'd have been in so much trouble. A true animal likely would have bitten her or made a lot of noise and gotten her caught. And why is she calling him a monster now?

Reborn as a Defective Drake: Snoweldon's Dragon

What happened to being a...a min-wyv or something?

"Oh, don't sulk. It's not like you can understand me," Cecily huffs but smiles at him.

Offense rises in him. If she can understand he's upset, she shouldn't think it's funny! And if he can't understand her, then why is she talking to him? Is talking to animals just something she does for the fun of it? Outraged, he picks himself up and looks around. He'll show her! He does understand! And he'll prove it!

The room he's been placed in is decorated in soft pastels. The bed he's been sitting upon reaches to the ceiling with its pastel pink canopy and green embroidered strands of dangling lace. The bedding beneath his claws is the same pastel pink but with blue accents. It surges plumply against his claws, as it appears to be stuffed with soft downy feathers to fight the cold. The bed sits catty-corner to one of the corners of the room with a desk spaced just down the wall. Both the bed and the other wooden furniture of the room gleam a dark, well-polished brown. In front and to the side of the bed, there's a little sitting area with plush couches, a dark wood coffee table, and several furs. Opposite the bed, a fireplace burns merrily, crafted from the same dark stone as the floor. Scattered about the room, pelts and rugs take up most of the walking area while a privacy screen separates the adjacent corner from the rest of the room. The little dragon can spy what he thinks is the edge of a large dresser peeking out from behind the dark,

Reborn as a Defective Drake: Snoweldon's Dragon

wooden screen.

At any rate, the paper the dragon seeks rests in a stack on the girl's desk.

Hopping up, he stumbles across the thick comforter on the bed to the edge. From here, the desk isn't but a foot away, but he's still not sure he can make that jump. Well, nothing ventured, nothing gained. Settling on his haunches since one of his front legs is rather useless, he wiggles a bit before launching himself from his back legs. For a moment, he feels like he's flying again, all wind and breathlessness rolled into one confusing but enlightening sensation.

And then his ribs make contact with the hard side of the desk, and he's scrabbling both for breath and for purchase on the smooth wood. Luckily, his claws are sharp, and he manages to hoist himself up at the expense of the desk's glossy finish. Lungs heaving in exertion, he barely slumps away from Cecily's hands as she reaches for him with an alarmed shout.

He spies an inkwell and some quills on her desk but no pencils or pens, so he scampers over to the ink and carefully balances on his injured leg to dip the claws of his other front leg into the inkwell. Hands come to lift him up and away, but he's already scratched out a word on the paper.

HI.

Short, but hopefully effective in attracting the little lady's attention.

"Hey! Be careful! You could have gotten hurt or broken

Reborn as a Defective Drake: Snoweldon's Dragon

my inkwell!" Cecily scolds him. "And look! You've gotten ink on yourself!" She holds him far from her body. "Where else have you gotten it?" Cecily grumbles to herself. Looking over the desk, she freezes at the sight of her paper. "Huh?" she asks.

She sets him down on her plumply cushioned chair, no longer caring for the ink on his claws. Luckily, the little dragon does care about the ink on his claw, and though it causes twinges to shoot up his injured shoulder, he balances carefully on his rump and one front leg. Cecily bends over the desk for a moment and then glances back at him.

"Mrrp!" He vocalizes and holds the ink-stained paw forward.

"You meant to get ink on just the paper. Because you knew that it was messy and that it went on paper?" she asks, narrowing her eyes at him and darting her pupils from his small, scaly form to the desk and back.

Making a low trill, the little dragon slowly lowers and raises his head a few times when he knows he's snatched her attention. Her sharp gasp and excited response tell him she's finally understood him.

"You can understand me?!" She cries loudly.

In response, he hisses and brings his tail to wiggle in front of his mouth in the universal 'Shhh!' motion. Cecily giggles in response and shakes her head.

"You're worried about being overheard," she whispers breathily as she gazes at him in awe.

Reborn as a Defective Drake: Snoweldon's Dragon

He huffs and repeats his 'Shhh!' motion. Again, the blonde girl only giggles.

"It's okay. This is the family wing; no one's allowed up here except family and personal attendants. I've just sent mine away. There's no one up here but us," Cecily says once she's stopped grinning. "But really, you can really understand me?"

Her blue eyes have gone huge with a mix of shock and awe, and he can see that this is something she finds highly incredulous. He can relate. It's not every day you wake up as a magical reptile in some kind of sub-dimension with sibling-eating monsters for family. Still, like a patient and understanding young dragon, he nods his head and holds out his paw to be cleaned. Surely, she wouldn't want him to get the ink on her chair? It's a very nice chair. He can attest to that much with how soft it feels underneath him. Meanwhile, Cecily is processing his answer.

"You really can understand me," she mutters. For a few moments, she stares at him before one small hand reaches to pinch the other arm. With a start, she jerks as if struck before surging forward to grab him.

"Eeek!" the little dragon shrieks as he's lifted.

Suddenly, he's being turned every which way and he finds himself facing the floor as she examines him.

"How is this possible? You're only a little monster. You shouldn't be capable of sentient thought," Cecily notes from above him. "Are you someone's familiar? I don't see a familiar

Reborn as a Defective Drake: Snoweldon's Dragon

bond, and there's no sign that you're a puppet. But...but you can't be intelligent on your own!" she declares after a lengthy investigation of his upturned body.

She likely would have continued except the little dragon had had quite enough of being poked and prodded. With a heave of his infantile abdominal muscles, he's twisting to sink his baby sharp fangs and claws into her pinky.

"Aaack!" Cecily shrieks and recoils with a sharp fling of her hand.

Luckily, it's at just the right angle to send him onto the bed instead of the floor. Unluckily, he hits the bed injured shoulder first, causing him to respond with a loud, discordant wail. Stars and white flash across his vision from the pain, and he lays there stunned for a good minute. In the background, he can hear a door opening and loud footsteps approaching a crying Cecily. There's a muffled conversation before the loud sounds of her gulping sobs eventually settle into a dizzy silence. But he doesn't really register that. Instead, he just gives a long pained whine from the burning in his shoulder. Being flung has ripped something or pulled it the exact wrong way as to cause it maximum pain. Either case, he isn't able to recollect much of anything until two warm, calloused hands curl around his form.

Something is said then. A word or a whisper or a wish of power. Something indefinite and unmeasurable confined in the space of a moment within the medium of compressed air

Reborn as a Defective Drake: Snoweldon's Dragon

forced from mortal lips.

And then it's like the world around him glows and the glow is entering him and filling up something empty. Bright, chilling ice crawls from the base of his neck along his spine like the slow but unstoppable growth of a glacier. The cold numbs his shoulder and other injuries in a strangely cleansing sensation. With his eyes closed, he can't tell much except that it's bright and that he feels as if the first frost of winter has delivered its blessing to his scales. And then, the chill recedes, leaving only the sensation of smooth, clean scales and a crisp, fresh breeze of winter's whispers.

Reborn as a Defective Drake: Snoweldon's Dragon

Blinking, the little dragon begins to breathe and see the world around him again as the glow of *something* fades into time. Looking up, he sees blue eyes the same colors as Cecily's. Only these eyes are set in a face far older, marked with the beginnings of crows' feet to the corners and dark eyelashes instead of blonde. A few wrinkles curl around a manly visage with soft, budding streaks of gray tangled into dark black strands. Though he has not seen this face before and has not heard it speak face to face, he somehow knows exactly where Cecily can trace her eyes to now.

Conwell Snoweldon, father of Cecily Snoweldon, acting Lord of Snoweldon, stares down at him with all of the emotion of a stone. And he, a small, insignificant, infant of a dragon, has just mauled the man's daughter.

This cannot end well.

The Lord of the Land and the (not a) Dragon

For a long moment, Lord Snoweldon and the dragon match eyes. But, the moment passes and the little dragon loses his nerve before squeezing his eyes shut with a whine. If he's going to die, he's certainly not going to be looking this man in the eyes. He's terrifying with such a blank face. However, instead of being met with death, he hears the sound of a deep chuckle. The man is laughing at him.

Blinking, he's met with the sight of old laugh lines falling into place with the smile on the dark-haired man's face. A little indignant at his fear being laughed at, he huffs and rolls over onto his stomach. Surely, if the man meant to kill him, he'd be dead by now. Pushing himself up, he's gratified to feel only the mildest of aches from his injured shoulder. Shifting his head, he lets out a chirp of astonishment at the sight of a red, slightly raised scar where he had once had fierce, red claw marks. The wound is gone! The man had made it go away, healed it like some kind of miracle worker! Turning, the little dragon begins chirping in a rush of squeaky, high pitched warbles.

"Thank you so much! It's healed! It's healed! Thank you!" he cries as loudly as he could, forgetting for a moment that he

can't speak the way he used to.

After a moment, he notices the trills and warbles he's been making and quiets down, but by then, it's too late. Cecily's giggling joins her father's now full-throated laughter.

"You're so cute!" she exclaims.

Like him, her wounds seem to have been healed, as he can't see any red on her hands. She clasps them together over her chest as if in a prayer, but her eyes remain glued to his small form. He shifts back, to the edge of Conwell's hands. If she tries to grab him again...he's had quite enough of that.

"Cecily, you're scaring him," Conwell murmurs. He'd gone quiet after a bit, but now the little dragon turns his attention back to the Snoweldon lord. Once more, he appears quite serious, but there's an amused gleam alight in his eyes. The man's upturned lips do nothing to disavow the dragon of the man's enjoyment of the situation.

"He's very young, despite his size. See how big his paws are compared to the rest of him? And how big his head is?" Conwell continues as he points out the dragon's various features. "He's probably only a few weeks old."

The dragon blinks, unsure of whether he's offended or not. He doesn't like being pointed at, but the man's not wrong about him being pretty young. This dragon body is only a day or two old. But how is this man familiar enough with his species to know any of this? Has he seen a dragon before?

"Huh? But he's as big as a min-wyv already." Cecily

gasps and her blue eyes widen to truly ridiculous proportions.

"Yes, but he's not a min-wyv. Indeed," Conwell frowns as he lifts the dragon slightly higher and examines him from a few different angles. "I'm not sure he's a part of the wyvern family at all. Wyverns only have the hind legs and their wings. They don't have another set of legs because they're primarily airbound creatures with their wings having the dual purpose of flight and supporting them on land. It gives them a unique wing structure but doesn't allow for adept ground mobility. As you can see, this little one's wings and front legs are two separate sets of limbs."

"But, if he's not a min-wyv, what is he?" Cecily asks in confusion. "We don't get any other scaly monsters around here. Mostly, we get furry ones that can take the winter cold. Certainly not smart ones." Here Cecily shoots him a dirty look, obviously remembering when he bit her from being held upside down.

"What is he, indeed..." Conwell eyes the little dragon contemplatively for a few moments longer.

The sharpness of his gaze is only just barely dulled by the sorrowful tilt of the man's eyebrows. He's sad for some reason, but he still appraises the while dragon seriously. The infantile dragon shifts a bit under the man's gaze. Somehow, he's pretty sure that Conwell knows exactly what he is. But for whatever reason, the man doesn't say anything regarding his species. Instead, with an air of gravity, he turns to his daughter.

Reborn as a Defective Drake: Snoweldon's Dragon

"Cecily, don't you have something to say to our guest?" Conwell prompts.

Cecily purses her lips but takes a step forward.

"I'm sorry I held you upside down and threw you," Cecily apologizes.

The dragon blinks.

"And?" Conwell prompts again.

Cecily huffs but acquiesces.

"I'm sorry for taking you into the castle without letting you choose and for stuffing you into my waist purse," Cecily admits sulkily.

Well, she should be.

The dragon huffs a bit but does incline his head in acceptance of her apology. It's not as if she had meant to hurt him. She appears to be a precocious child, as inquisitive as she is rash.

"Yes, you should be. Monsters, even small ones like this one, are very dangerous, Cecily. Even a miniature wyvern could kill someone, though their species has been socialized and bred for docility towards humans," Conwell lectures.

Meanwhile, the little dragon listens closely.

Monsters? Like, the classification from an RPG game, or something? Not like, monster as in a person doing monstrous things, but as in an actual type of creature.

But, if he's a monster, then what's to stop a rabbit from being a monster? Obviously, it doesn't have wings or spit fire, but he doesn't think all of the other monsters do either? The giant chicken monster back in the forest didn't fly with its wings, and it didn't seem to be able to spit fire. Just...eat things in a macabre and awfully scary way.

"But he's friendly," Cecily says plaintively.

Conwell sighs and shakes his head a little.

"Yes, but others would not be. Even the miniature wyverns kept for sending messages are handled rarely and with heavy, protective gloves. This one..." Here Conwell side-eyes the small, white scaled reptile sitting in his cupped hands. "This one's unique amongst all others of its kind."

"He is?" Cecily asks and peers closely at the little dragon once more. Though safe in Conwell's hands, the dragon shifts uneasily a bit. "How? He's just like an icey min-wyv but with legs."

Conwell shifts, and the little dragon turns to see the man gazing down solemnly once more.

"Well, he's...he's a bit different from others." Conwell haltingly explains.

He looks between his child and the infantile dragon in his hands again before coming to some sort of internal decision. Meanwhile, the little dragon perks up. Does Conwell know why his family tried to kill him?

"He's a very special kind of monster, Cecily. See how he doesn't have spikes the way a miniature wyvern would?"

"Uh-huh," Cecily nods and reaches out to run a gentle

finger along his spine. "He's soft and smooth."

The little dragon trills a little at the pleasant touch.

Oooh, that feels good! But, no spikes? Like his siblings?

He looks over his shoulders and sees a smooth, bumpy area but no spikes.

Huh, were those important for something?

"And, do you see how bright of a white he is? He doesn't have any color variation at all. Which, for his kind, is highly unusual."

His siblings had all been black, so that fits. Conwell seemed to be avoiding calling him a dragon though. Perhaps there's a reason for that? The little dragon tilts his head to the side and ponders as he continues to listen.

"It is? But he looks just like a min-wyv? And they're white."

"Yes, but only in some places, and they're typically only a milky-white if they're miniature ice wyverns. Most miniature wyverns will have some gray or blue on their underbelly and spikes. It differentiates males from females and helps them, ah, have kids." Here Conwell halts awkwardly before forging onwards. "Anyway, not even ice wyverns are actually pure white, they just look like it. Among all of monster-kind, there's not a single monster that's actually colored entirely white. This is due to the fact that the color white is only created when an object is rejecting almost all outside magic and light. Rather, it reflects it back at the world around it. People just perceive it as white because we can't understand what we're actually looking at." Conwell rubs a thumb along the dragon's body, careful but sure in his movement.

The little dragon is quite confused, though. His siblings absorb magic? Is that why they had been so big and strong and why he'd been so small? He looks over his white skin again with a frown across his snout. Does being unable to absorb magic mean he'll stay small or something? Or can his siblings do magic, and he can't? It's frustrating to have so many questions popping up about himself when he can't even ask them himself. What does being unable to absorb magic mean for him?

"So, other monsters can absorb light and magic, but he doesn't?" Cecily asks.

The little dragon pays rapt attention, now that the conversation was on something so useful and important.

"Yes. Because of his skin color, he can't absorb as much of the natural mana of the air. It's, well, I suppose, it could be called a birth defect among monsters, being born without the ability to absorb mana."

The little dragon sighs. He's just got the worst luck.

"Like cousin Larskson?" Cecily questions curiously.

"Yes, like your cousin. Yet, somehow, no one's really sure how, but monsters such as these gain a special power: they can be as smart as humans or any other sentient race. In some cases, they can rival even the elves with their ability to

Reborn as a Defective Drake: Snoweldon's Dragon

learn and understand. Because of this, we call these monsters Sages, as among their kind, they are far wiser and more intelligent."

He blinks at the new information. A Sage? He's a Sage? It feels so grandiose for someone who'd just started college. But he supposes dying and being reborn might have something to do with it. Were other Sages people who'd died and been reborn too? Was the intelligence due to being reborn, or due to the birth defect he'd been born with? He didn't feel any smarter or dumber, so he's not sure if his intelligence could have been affected.

It's a little scary to think about, not being himself but not being able to tell. So instead, he pushes it out of his head and into a box marked "figure out later." He needs to know more from this conversation right now, not ponder his loss or gain of intelligence.

"So he's really smart?" Cecily asks.

"Yes. He's probably smarter than even you and I," Conwell intones seriously.

He preens a little at the praise. It's nice to be called smart. Meanwhile, Cecily then tilts her head in confusion.

"But father, if he rejects all outside mana, then how did you heal him?" The dragon blinks. That's a...very astute question coming from a small child. But, Cecily was a very curious child, wasn't she?

"Well, the first reason is that the resistance to magic is

Reborn as a Defective Drake: Snoweldon's Dragon

only present in the top layer of his skin. When he's cut or hurt badly enough to split the skin, magic can be applied through the wound to the rest of his body.The second reason is that he's still very young, and his skin is still thin and baby soft. If he were to grow up, he would have thick skin capable of repelling massive amounts of magic. It would allow him to be immune to most magical attacks."

Good to know, the little dragon thinks to himself.

Maybe not absorbing magic from the air wasn't such a bad thing after all. He sniffs daintily and considers it before deciding that he still doesn't know enough about what his body does with mana to be happy or sad that he doesn't absorb it. Being immune to attack magic sounds cool, but he's still tiny and weak compared to his litter (or was it hatch?)mates.

"Oh, so because he's a baby he can still absorb a little bit of magic?" Cecily blinks and furrows her eyebrows together.

Despite having the answer to her question, it does not appear that she's quite happy with it.

"That's correct, Cecily," Conwell answers approvingly.

"But, if he's still a baby, where're his parents? Don't his mom and dad care that he was hurt?"

Here Conwell winces. He carefully maneuvers himself onto the bed with the little dragon in his lap. He pats the bed and waits till Cecily plops down beside him before he starts speaking again. The infant dragon blinks in confusion. Is Conwell concerned for him and Cecily? Why?

Reborn as a Defective Drake: Snoweldon's Dragon

"That's another issue with Sages, Cecily. Other monsters can tell that they are...different. In most species, when a sage is born, the family of the sage will kill or...eat the sage." Gently, with the care of the first frost on blades of grass, he rubs his fingers soothingly over the little dragon's back.

It's soothing but doesn't help the little reptile's confusion or frown until he hears and sees Cecily's reaction.

"His parents would eat him?!" she cries out in horror.

Tears spring to her eyes, and the healthy blush on her face fades to the white of a near corpse. She looks at him from tearful blue eyes as if he's the most fragile and priceless glass trinket she's ever seen.

"Why?" she gasps out. "Why would they hurt their baby? Don't they love him?"

Conwell sighs and loops an arm over his daughter's shoulder to pull her close. Cecily responds by burrowing into her father's side.

Oh...this was why Conwell thought Cecily and he would be upset. Because any child who'd been nearly murdered and eaten by their siblings would be traumatized by the experience. He...didn't really know what he felt about that. Either being almost murdered by his own siblings or the idea that they would have eaten him. Both are pretty horrible, and he hasn't really had time to come to terms with it all yet. The last forty-eight hours or so have happened so quickly that he hasn't really had time to think. He's been going from one bad

Reborn as a Defective Drake: Snoweldon's Dragon

situation to the next without any room to breathe.

Being almost murdered by his siblings had been scary, but so had everything else. Also, it wasn't as if that had been his first moments of life when he remembered life as a human. He'd had other memories to draw on to keep him moving, though some of that could just be shock. Even now, this life doesn't feel quite real, more a bad dream than a waking memory.

"Monsters aren't like humans, Cecily. They don't form emotional attachments like we do. For them, the only difference between family members and outsiders is their appearance. Because this little one doesn't look like he should, they won't regard him as one of their own. To other monsters, he is an anomaly or abomination," Conwell explains. Cecily sniffles into the man's side but doesn't speak as her father continues. "That's why it's going to be very important for you to take good care of him."

The little dragon blinks. Cecily looks up.

"*What*?!" He barks.

His eyes widen to impossible sizes as he comes to terms with what Conwell has just implied.

"What do you mean, Father?" Cecily asks, unknowingly mirroring the little dragon's own query.

"Why, exactly what I said, Cecily." Conwell smiles down at his daughter. "You've found a Sage, a rare, friendly monster that only appears once every thousand years. So long as you

Reborn as a Defective Drake: Snoweldon's Dragon

respect him and are good to him, he will not harm you. In fact, I think the two of you could become good friends. Perhaps you were meant to be friends."

The Snoweldon Lord is offering for the little dragon to stay with Cecily? In the fort? And be fed and taken care of? But the man had just been saying how dangerous monsters are?

"Yes, but... I thought monsters weren't allowed in the fort."

"They aren't, and you do need to remember not to go picking up small ones and bringing them inside." Here, the man gives Cecily an especially unimpressed look.

The girl pouts a bit and looks towards the windows in an effort not to meet her father's eyes.

After a moment, Conwell continues, "He'll be a special case. He's going to be smaller and weaker than other monsters. If he's not taken care of, I don't think he'll survive. And with his intelligence, I doubt he's going to cause trouble on purpose."

Here, Conwell gives the little dragon a look. It's not necessarily threatening, but it is stern; so, the little dragon hurries to nod his head.

He'll behave if that means he gets to eat and sleep here in the fort. Honestly, this is almost too good to be true! After everything that's happened, this feels to be an impossible stroke of good fortune.

"Furthermore, Sages are rare, Cecily. You'll only meet one once in your life if you're very, very lucky or if fate wills it.

Reborn as a Defective Drake: Snoweldon's Dragon

Becoming friends with him, learning from each other...I believe it will be a once in a millennium experience that was given to you for a reason."

"So, he can stay? I can keep him?" Cecily asks, beginning to become excited.

"You won't be keeping him, Cecily. He's as smart as you or I; there is no keeping of a sentient being," Conwell objects. "But you will be taking care of him. He's one of the rarest beings in history; you should get to know him and learn from him while you can. He's naturally weaker and smaller than other monsters. You'll have to take good care of him, but only if he agrees."

"I will father, I will!" Cecily pledges heartily. She smiles brightly, and her wide eyes belie her joy. Conwell looks down at the dragon in his lap, and it doesn't take him saying anything for the little dragon to understand that the Snoweldon Lord is waiting for the dragon's acceptance. Without hesitance, he gives a high, happy trill. Turning, he huddles back on his haunches for a moment before leaping over to Cecily's lap. He digs his claws into the soft material of her apron skirt to balance himself and looks up into her surprised blue irises.

"Oh!" Cecily gasps before bringing her hands around to steady him.

She's careful not to constrict him, but he appreciates the help. Lap jumping should be made an olympic sport; it's very hard to maintain balance.

Reborn as a Defective Drake: Snoweldon's Dragon

"Well, then. I think it's been decided. Our new friend will be staying with us," Conwell announces. And like that, he's somehow gone from forty-eight hours of trying not to die to being given food, shelter, and safety. Goodness, it's been rough.

Of Plumbing and Early Mornings

The two are put to bed shortly afterwards. Despite finding one of the rarest creatures in the world, schooling waits for no one. Since the little dragon is going to be Cecily's responsibility, he's apparently going to be going to lessons with her.

Still, he isn't the least bit upset. Conwell had left to speak to his wife, but servants had come with smoked ham and water for the little dragon. It had been delicious, and he's not just talking about the meat. That water had been the first water he'd actually been able to have in this life, and it had tasted so sweet, he'd just about choked himself trying to lap it out of the bowl. Afterwards, Cecily's mother had had a few sharp words with her daughter on the practice of bringing baby monsters home. He hadn't really heard much of it, as he'd conked out on some pelts near the fireplace. He hadn't meant to, but the crackling flames had been so warm and soothing that they had lulled his exhausted, infantile body to sleep.

Now it's early morning, and the flames that had flared so strongly with bright golden hues the night before have burned down to orange and red-rimmed coals. The coals are

Reborn as a Defective Drake: Snoweldon's Dragon

still warm but only give off a faint glow. Blinking, the little dragon sits up slowly and arches his back luxuriously. He feels a few bones pop and sighs in contentment. He feels well-rested and healthy; the aches and pains of yesterday have fled with the coming of dawn. Looking towards Cecily's large, collumned windows and balcony, he can just barely see the creeping of the morning sun's faint rays. The horizon is dusted in soft amber, but no burning star has yet peeked over the horizon.

Pushing himself up, he sniffs and breathes in the scent of faint smoke alongside flowers and ink. Padding softly, he sets out to explore the room more thoroughly. As he had noticed last night, Cecily's bed is a large canopy bed of pastel colors. It sits perpendicular to a corner with the desk along one of the walls adjacent to it. One of the wide, columned windows rests to the otherside of the bed, giving Cecily what is likely one of the best views in the fort.

The sitting area takes up the center of the room, and the dragon is amused to see the edges of papers, books, and odd little objects peeking over the edges of the sofas and coffee table. Despite the clean desk, it seems Cecily can be a bit of a mess. Scampering over, he looks up at the edges of the papers in curiosity. What do noble children learn here in this strange world? Do they learn poetry, music, and philosophy like many had in his old world?

He's not nearly tall enough to get a good look at it though. For all his intellect, he stands at only a few inches tall. The furniture towers above him and holds the pages high above his head. Giving a sigh and a shake of his head, he turns to go amuse himself elsewhere. It's too early to wake Cecily, but he's awake and bored.

Trotting over to the corner, he peers behind the privacy screen. As expected, Cecily's wardrobe and dresser hug the walls. As unexpected, an ivory colored tub with golden feet rests in the center of the hidden corner. A pipe even extends from the ground to wrap round the side and pour into the bath. Do they have running water here? Sniffing, he approaches the tub and nudges his nose around the base of the pipe. The scent of water, something he could only describe as 'wet' and that he had learned the night before, greets him.

He blinks. They do have running water. Incredible! Did it come heated? He looks for a way to get on top of the tub and spots a footstool. It's one of those nice, step ones that allow a person to step up in increments. Nodding to himself, he hurries over to push it closer to the tub. Unfortunately, not only is it quite heavy, but it also makes a squeaky noise on the stone floor when it moves. Pausing, the little dragon listens carefully to see if he has woken Cecily. He doesn't think she'll get mad at him for exploring and looking at the tub, but he'd rather not wake her up. If she's not an early morning person, he'd rather not find out on his first day with her.

Still, he doesn't hear anything. Bobbing his head to himself, he finishes the arduous task of scooting the step-stool to the edge of the tub. Sitting back, he looks up at the first step.

Reborn as a Defective Drake: Snoweldon's Dragon

He can make that. He crouches and waggles his haunches as he bunches his muscles. Then, he springs forward and is just able to get his front legs and some of his chest over the edge of the step. His rear and tail dangle off the edge behind them. Straining, he claws at the wood with his hind legs and heaves himself over the edge. Panting, he looks back over the edge to see that the floor isn't too far away, but he's still proud of his accomplishment. Unfortunately, he might have scraped the finish off the stool with his claws.

Oops.

After a moment, he glances at the next step. It's the same distance up as the first had been; so, he knows he can make it. He crouches and springs up again. This time he manages to get most of   himself over the edge of the step and only has to work a little bit more to get the rest of himself up. Peering up, he sees the lip of the tub rising imperiously above him. It's a few inches farther above his head than the steps had been. Still, he has questions about the availability of hot water that will not be denied.

So, girding himself for the herculean task ahead, he creeps back towards the edge of the step and crouches down. He breathes in deeply, wiggles a little to get the best grip possible on the wood beneath him, and bounds forward into a springing jump. His claws just breach the edge, and then, he's hanging precariously from the rim of the tub.

Oh... This might have been a bad idea, he thinks to himself.

Still, he claws at the tub with his hind legs to try to boost himself up. It works somewhat; with some loud 'nail on chalkboard' noises, he is able to push his head and chest over the lip of the tub. Sadly, due to the angle of the lip of the tub and the walls of it, once he's at that stage, he can no longer reach the wall of the tub with his hind legs. Straining, he tries to pull himself forward using his front legs, but he can't get enough upward motion to pull himself up.

He's stuck. This was definitely not the brightest idea he's ever had. Still, from here he can see the pipe as it feeds into the faucet which means he can tell that... he can't tell if it has hot water or not. There aren't any obvious knobs at the base of the faucet, but there are two odd cylinders of metal that jut out about an inch from the base. The cylinders are placed where bath knobs would be placed normally but lack any way to turn them that the young dragon can see. Instead, what he can see is a strange character inscribed upon the flat end of the cylinders. One is a series of circles within each other while the other is several jagged lines intercepting one another.

It's strange, but not as strange as the fact that the symbols and cylinders appear to be glowing. The circle-themed symbol glows deep blue while the jagged-line symbol glows a red-orange. He tilts his head in curiosity at the sight. He'd seen mostly medieval-age styles and items in town, so this isn't likely to be any sort of machine or science. Thus, that means that it must be magic.

Excitement builds within him. He knows that magic exists in this new world. But he hasn't really had a chance to mess with it yet. And if magic can give him a bath full of hot water...

He's just about ready for another attempt at pulling himself over the lip of the tub when small fingers close around his tiny form.

"And just what do you think you're doing?" Cecily Snoweldon asks as she scoops him up.

Her blonde hair sits mussed on her head, and he can still spot the crusty green of the Sandman's visit in her eyes. She's probably just woken up.

Oops.

He must have woken her trying to get over the lip of the tub. Still, nothing to do about it now.

He points one front paw at the tub and chirps. Cecily tilts her head and looks at the tub and then back at him.

"You were curious about my tub?" She asks him.

He trills happily and nods his head. She furrows her brow at his answer.

"Why? It's just a tub," she huffs and then sets him down just beyond the privacy screen. "You woke me up so early, I might as well get the bath I missed yesterday."

Reborn as a Defective Drake: Snoweldon's Dragon

Welp.

He's definitely not going to get his answer now. Giving an irritated look at the privacy screen, he turns to survey the room once more.

There's not really anything else of interest. Cecily has several large wooden chests lining the walls, but he doesn't really feel like invading her privacy, and he doubts he could get into them anyway. With a sigh, he pads over to the pelts in front of the fire to settle down once again. He is a little tired after all that effort, and there's nothing better to do but doze. Breathing calmly, he listens as Cecily turns on her water. It plops into the tub heavily and he smiles at the thought of how good the water pressure sounds.

Cecily starts humming when she gets in, so it can't be cold water. If it isn't heated, he doubts she'd be very happy about getting a bath. The water in the fountain had been freezing, and that water had been warmed by the sun. So, the fort most likely has heated water. He doesn't know how he got so lucky, but he hopes his luck holds. For a few minutes, he just rests there, content to be warmed by the coals in the fireplace and lulled by Cecily's melodic humming.

The door opens, and he looks up to see a woman with brown, curly hair come in. She is dressed in a rosy-red dress and a white apron. A white bonnet holds her roiling curls at bay. In her arms, she holds a tray full of food and a tea kettle. Behind her, a young blonde boy follows. He's dressed in brown breaches and a red vest but holds a basket of firewood. The maid goes to the sitting area and begins moving things around. He can't see it, but he can hear her shifting Cecily's papers and things to make room for the tray and tea.

Meanwhile, the boy with the firewood walks towards the fireplace, only to freeze when he notices the dragon. He gasps loudly and steps back a few terrified steps. The firewood in his arms drops with a loud clatter. The little dragon tilts his head and gives a concerned trill.

"Lorca, what-?" The maid turns towards the noise with a half uttered reprimand already passing her lips but also stops at the sight of the little dragon. Her brown eyes widen to epic proportions and all of the blood leaves her face. "By golly, there's a monster in here!" she gasps out.

Her thin hands flutter in front of her uselessly before she collapses in a dead faint. Luckily, she's in just the right position to end up partially on one of the couches instead of the floor. The thump she makes as she hits it, combined with the previous clatter of the firewood, is apparently enough to get Cecily's attention though. The baby fire-breather blinks and glances behind him but doesn't see anything particularly scary. Don't tell him...were they afraid of him?

"Alya, Lorca? Is something the matter?" the girl calls from behind the partitioned bathing area.

Water sloshes about, and it seems as if she gets out when the sound of dripping water on stone can be heard.

Reborn as a Defective Drake: Snoweldon's Dragon

"L-Lady Cecily. Y-you n-need to run! There's a monster in here!" Lorca cries out.

His freckled face has gone starkly white in fright, but he valiantly grabs a piece of firewood and holds it aloft like a weapon. The little dragon stares nonplussed for a moment as it dawns on him that these servants really are afraid of him. Him, a small reptile of only a few inches and a lifespan measuring in days. It's more than a little off putting. Honestly, it's as absurd as being afraid of earth snakes or garter snakes.

"A monster?" Cecily asks, confused. "Oh, you mean the Sage. It's okay. Father said he's going to be my responsibility from now on. We're supposed to become friends and he's going to live with me."

Wood scrapes together as Cecily opens a drawer on her dresser.

"Say, is Alya there? I need her help getting dressed. I can't reach all the buttons in the back." Cecily asks.

Unfortunately, Cecily's words seem to be the final straw for young Lorca as the boy soon faints as well. The little dragon winces at the sound of the boy's head hitting the ground. Ouch. That was going to smart when he woke up.

"Lorca? Alya?" Cecily calls. She walks to the edge of the partition and peeks around the edge. For a moment, she just stares at the room before her. Her servants lay passed out on the floor and couch while her new monster friend sits innocently in front of the hearth.

Reborn as a Defective Drake: Snoweldon's Dragon

"Er, Little Sage, did something happen?" Cecily asks incredulously.

"Mrrp?" the little dragon articulates, with a confuzzled shrug of his shoulders.

It seems that the common people aren't nearly as level-headed around monsters as the nobility are. He stands and pads over to sniff at Lorcas. The boy smells like rich pines and smoke. He must spend a lot of time fetching wood and stoking fires.

That's his job? To keep all the fires in the keep going?

It doesn't seem like something that should take up a person's whole day, but he can imagine that if the boy also has to cut the wood, as suggested by his woody, sappy scent, it could then be a very time-consuming task.

He's interrupted from his thoughts by the reappearance of Cecily. Today, she's wearing a white dress with a light blue-and-green skirt and vest. For some reason, she seems to be pouting. He trots over to her and paws at her foot when she sits down on the couch to eat.

"Oh, are you hungry too?" she asks him after she takes a bite of croissant.

He is, but that's not why he was nudging her. Still, he's grateful when she cups him in her hands and lifts him onto the coffee table beside the tray. He's sat on top of some papers, but he doesn't care to look at them in favor of carefully pawing at Cecily's hand when she goes to pour herself some tea.

Reborn as a Defective Drake: Snoweldon's Dragon

"What? You can pick what you like. I don't mind," Cecily mutters in irritation as she gestures to her breakfast spread.

The breakfast she's been served has a basket of warm, freshly baked scones and croissants, a plate of scrambled eggs and bacon, and some smoked ham. It's far too much for a child, but he supposes that's just what happens when you serve breakfast to nobility. Still, he wants to know what's upset her so much. She seems inordinately frustrated about something.

Huffing a little, he hops forward and throws himself atop Cecily's wrist.

"Hey!" Cecily cries.

"Scrrk!" He makes a high pitched shriek to catch her attention.

Then, he nuzzles his snout into her arm, catching the scent of rose hips and maybe some cinnamon.

"You don't want breakfast?" Cecily asks.

The white reptile looks up and shakes his head before leaning down to nuzzle at her wrist again.

"You want...me to..." Cecily's brow furrows as she tries to understand what her new draconic companion wants from her.

Giving a sigh, the little dragon looks up and makes some exaggerated trilling noises while bobbing his head. Then, he makes some angry upset noises and buries his head under his paws.

"You want to know why I'm upset?" Cecily asks in surprise.

He nods his head eagerly. Yes, he wants to know why the little lady is upset.

"Oh, that's because Maester Dorian doesn't like it when I don't wear the proper attire for my exercise lessons. Unfortunately, all of those dresses have buttons in the back, but since Alya has fainted, I won't be able to wear one. That means I'll miss my exercise lesson, and I like those. Maester Dorian always teaches such interesting things," Cecily explains. "He's supposed to just be teaching me dance, but he says the footwork from dance is a good base for swordplay or fighting, and Father doesn't mind when he teaches me some of those. So long as mother doesn't find out, I'm allowed to learn how to defend myself. He's also teaching me to move like he does and jump around high places. He calls it the Cat's Walk. It's a lot of fun." Cecily grins and leans over him conspiratorially. "Can you imagine it, Little Sage? Me, jumping from rooftop to rooftop like some sort of rogue or assassin! It'd be so cool!" she whispers excitedly.

Then, her expression falls and she looks back at her clothes for the day.

"He'll never let me practice my jumps today, though. He'll make me dance with Sanders instead. It's going to be so dull," she grumbles glumly.

Reborn as a Defective Drake: Snoweldon's Dragon

Humming, the little dragon nuzzles her wrist and gives his own grin upwards. Her eyes lighten as she catches the meaning of his actions.

"Oh, you're right. Today can't be that boring! I have you to take with me!" Cecily exclaims in excitement.

Nodding to both himself and the little lady, the white reptile slides off her wrist and heads towards the ham. He's quite famished. Getting into trouble, scaring the servants, and keeping the noble child happy is hard work, you know.

Lorca and Alya do wake before the pair leaves for their lessons, but only just. Lorca wakes first, and for a moment, he just stares at the ceiling, confused. At the time, Cecily had just finished grabbing her things and stuffing them irreverently into a leather over-the-shoulder bag. The white reptile watches her attentively from his place on the coffee table.

Most of the books she's stuffing into her bag appear to be handwritten and bound in leather; they bear no sign of a printing press. Frowning, he's about to jump down to prepare to follow Cecily out the door when Lorcas begins groaning. The lad shifts about restlessly for a moment before bolting upright with a violent intake of air. Glancing about, Lorca doesn't see Cecily hastily slinging her backpack on her shoulders or the little Sage jumping onto the girl's outstretched hands.

Somehow, it seems they are of one mind when it comes to dramatically fainting servants: leave them be. As it is, the servant only glances back as Cecily opens one of the wooden double doors to her room and slides through. His startled cry dies as the way is blocked by the heavy fir door. Looking up, the dragon chirps his approval and is surprised but very happy

Reborn as a Defective Drake: Snoweldon's Dragon

to see Cecily already smiling down mischievously. Despite her nobility and mother, she has a bit of an impish side to her.

Glancing about, the little dragon takes note of their surroundings. He hadn't been able to see it all last night, being stuck in Cecily's coin purse, but now he finds himself in awe of the ancient masonry around him. It's clearly limestone, as it lacks the sheen of marble and is too varied in color to be just stone. Soft green and yellow spots break up the monotony of brown and gray bricks while wide, collumned windows take up the opposite side of the hall. Because the stone beneath Cecily's feet only comes in gray, he supposes they used normal stone for that. Most of the hall is covered by large, woven wool rugs, likely to keep in heat more than keep dirt from being tracked. Likewise, large tapestries hang from the walls on either side of Cecily's door.

Adjacent to Cecily's door, several other doors are spaced evenly down the hall, likely leading to the other family members' bedrooms. The hall's large size seems wasteful for only holding bedrooms, but the view from the windows deserves as much. Even as Cecily begins traversing down the hall, he can still make out the awe-inspiring view of the valley below. These windows look out onto the far side of the grounds away from the city. So instead of looking out at the hustle and bustle of a waking medieval city, he's greeted with the sight of fir-covered blue mountains, morning mists, and bright green fields that arc down into a mist-veiled valley.

Reborn as a Defective Drake: Snoweldon's Dragon

Apparently, the fort rests on the crest of a mountain's foothill with the city in the lesser valley, and the steeper valley behind the fort.

Cecily ignores the view, probably used to it considering she lives here; but for the little dragon, he only gets a few tantalizing moments to stare at the marvels of nature before Cecily carries him to a grand, spiraling staircase. Here, one could expect to come across artistic embellishments or gratuitous ornamentation, but instead the staircase is carved of the same stone as the floor with pillars of different colored sandstone framing the way. It's rustic and simple; though a little confused at how plain the fort is, the little dragon likes it somehow. It matches the people here, with the women's rich colored aprons and the men's simple vests or overcoats.

So far, he hasn't really seen anything as overt as what he'd been expecting when brought into the ruling noble's home. He sees no greek corinthian pillars or flamboyant gothic windows. He hasn't seen any stained glass or cast iron decorations. Instead, he has seen some colored limestone, unadorned pillars similar to Roman Tuscan pillars but lacking even the minimal rings of the capital or base, and now, a staircase defined by dark timber and ageless stone. It's all very rustic. All it's missing is some fashionable wood paneling and modern glass, and it could be almost viewed as a modern mountain retreat or something!

Cecily walks down three flights of stairs before she gets off the staircase. To the dragon's surprise, the stairs continue down into the depths, though he's quite certain they've arrived at the ground floor already. A cellar, or a dungeon maybe? That'd be cool to explore!

Still, he doesn't think about it for long, as Cecily enters the main hall of the fort, and he finds himself looking with interest at the multitude of pelts and weapons that hang on the walls: trophies and warnings both. A throne sits on one end of the hall, carved of dark wood and adorned with pelts. Currently, the Snoweldon Lord occupies it with his slim figure and dark hair. He waves at Cecily as she passes but doesn't look away from the small group of important-looking people he's conversing with or the papers in his hands. Various employees, soldiers, and even a few nobles can be seen going about their daily toils. Most of them take no notice of Cecily, though the few she passes close to tend to curtsey or bow in respect for her status. The ones who notice the dragon resting on the noble girl appear shocked and confused, but Cecily pays them no mind. She strides past them confidently and heads down a side passage filled with old portraits of dark-haired people. Then, she heads to a single, light wooden door and knocks twice before entering.

"Greetings, Maester Theodore," she says with a curtsey. Meanwhile, the little dragon finds himself gaping at a small room packed floor to ceiling with a maddening mix of paperwork and books. They cover the walls, shelves, and any available surface. It's as if a small library has been transported into the confines of the room.

Reborn as a Defective Drake: Snoweldon's Dragon

"Hello and good morning, my young lady Cecily," a wizened old man greets from behind the book-strewn desk.

He wears dark colored breeches and a white tunic but has thrown his blue vest over the back of his chair. He peers at Cecily through cloud-blue eyes and a set of gold-wired spectacles. Then, he turns his attention down to the little dragon.

"And hello to you, as well, my young friend," he murmurs with a bright gleam to his eyes.

The man seems oddly fascinated with the dragon, and his fingers twitch as though wishing to write something down. It's a little disconcerting for the dragon, and he shifts in Cecily's hands uneasily.

"I'm Theodore Markwin, Historian and Elder of Snoweldon. It's a pleasure and an honor to meet such a unique existence and be your instructor in history." Theodore dips his head, and the little dragon feels obliged to give an uncomfortable chirp back.

It feels far more grandiose than it perhaps should be, this man's greeting and his seeming expectations for the infant dragon.

Cecily looks down at him with a raised, blonde brow but does seem to pick up on his discomfort. Perhaps it was the way he had started digging his claws into her arms?

Reborn as a Defective Drake: Snoweldon's Dragon

"Shall we begin the lesson, Maester Theodore?" she asks primly, sweeping the odd moment under the rug by way of poise and manners.

"Er-erm, yes, milady." Surprised eyes glance back at Cecily as if only just remembering her presence. "Have a seat, and I'll begin the lesson. We just spoke of the Adarian wars in the fourth and fifth centuries. These wars, if you'll remember, centered on obtaining focus stones as a resource, as whoever obtained them held the most military might. This was before Johan Mavern discovered how to synthesize focus crystals using the remains of monster corpses. When he discovered how to synthesize focus cores in the fifth century, he published his techniques in a book called *The 59 Uses of Monster Bodies*."

"Thanks to this, wars dedicated to obtaining focus gems died down, as countries began focusing on scientific goals instead of making war with one another. The next fifty years are known as the 'Illumination of the Wizeen'." The man abruptly begins the lesson without waiting for Cecily to take a seat.

With a soft sigh, she sets him down on a nearby tower of books and takes a seat on the only chair left bare of parchment or leather-bound tomes.

Pulling out a leather notebook, she grabs a quill and ink jar to begin note-taking. She seems to have expected this kind of beginning to the lesson and even seems to find the topic of discussion a little boring, nibbling on the end of her quill and

Reborn as a Defective Drake: Snoweldon's Dragon

lacklusterly jotting down notes as she pleases. Meanwhile, the baby dragon cocks his head to the side, unfamiliar with the topics being recited. Focus gems? Adorian wars? He shuffles for a moment when Theodore begins talking of using monster cores to create what must be a usually scarce resource.

I'm lucky I was reborn as a Sage, the little lizard muses to himself. He'd rather not be ground up to create whatever a focus gem was. Still, what is a focus gem? It's obviously valuable and probably a type of mineral? He's never heard of a mineral that can be synthesized by organic matter though...

"The Illumination Era was the first time focus cores could be distributed beyond the rich or military. This allowed commoners to use magic for their daily lives,making obtaining food for themselves much easier. This rise in wealth ended what we refer to as the Dark Ages. Now, when did the Dark Ages begin, Lady Cecily?" Theodore asks.

"Er-" Cecily pauses, and a brief panicky look overtakes her countenance. "I can't remember, Maester Theodore," Cecily admits with a polite smile.

Theodore smiles back, but gives a brief chuckle.

"That's because it didn't start. We don't actually have any reliable records of that far back. The Dark Ages began before the Ilvum calendar was finalized and long before our writing systems grew from ideograms to an actual alphabet. Technically, we don't have any solid proof that the continent wasn't always going through such poverty, just a few pointers

Reborn as a Defective Drake: Snoweldon's Dragon

that might suggest lost wealth or knowledge," Theodora explains.

"But if we don't have actual proof, why are you so sure, Maester Theodore?" Cecily asks.

She frowns in a way that looks more like a pout due to her young age, but it was likely meant to be firm.

"Why, because we live in one such piece of proof," Theodore says joyously. "Snoweldon castle is much older than the Ilvum calendar and the Ilvum writing system. I'd say it's at least as old as the Corpheonus groups, but they left their mark on everything they touch, and I haven't seen a lick of their sigils. Honestly, how do you think you get your bathwater or heat your stone floors in the winter?"

"By magic?" Cecily asks, confused.

"Well, I would hope so." He peers over his glasses at her. "But what kind of magic?"

"I-I don't know?"

"Sigil magic. Or Enchanting. Whichever term you want to use. The Corpheonus groups were known for their ability to bind magic commands and even magic to common items. Usually, an item would need to be of magic to maintain or hold magic, but the Corpheonus groups each found separate ways to imbue normal items with magic and its effects. In this case, the Corpheonus Snoweld group that eventually became known as the Snowelds enchanted the fort with magic to make drawing water easier and to allow better insulation for the cold climate.

Reborn as a Defective Drake: Snoweldon's Dragon

There could be other enchantments left behind, but we would never know, seeing as much of the knowledge of enchantments was destroyed in the Ilvum purges." Theodore sighs gustily at the end of his explanation. "Honestly, those ruffians. I'd love to go back and give them a good speaking to about destroying history just because they don't like it." the old man utters angrily.

He fumes silently for a moment, and the little dragon takes the time to chirp inquisitively from his spot on the books.

"Little Sage?" Cecily questions as she looks over.

However, the baby dragon just tilts his head at Theodore. If the man's too upset to lecture, maybe he could cue him into explaining some things? Like, the Ilvum people? Or the purge? That sounded like something important if it'd destroyed so much history.

"Oh, I suppose you're quite curious aren't you? You don't have the breadth of knowledge Cecily has from previous lessons. Despite your superior intellect, you still need some background information." The historian looks over at the Sage with a smile, clearly over his anger at the Ilvum people. It's rather jolting, the man's fascination and subsequent change in temperament.

It's also uncomfortable, the way the man has set the infant dragon on some sort of mental pedestal. He's not sure he'll be able to live up to the man's high expectations or even if he wants to. He chirps, wanting the man to give some context to the history lesson that he'd been giving Cecily.

"Well, first things first, let's get out a map. You'll have a hard time figuring out all of the countries and power struggles if you don't understand what our geography looks like. Cecily, since this should just be review for you, you'll be the one to name capitals, ruling powers, and political contention," Theodore announces as he stands to begin rooting around on the bookshelf behind him. The next time period is filled with Cecily going over an abbreviated history of the region.

~   ~   ~

"How come he gets the simple version?" Cecily asks grumpily.

Evidently, she did not like having to learn whatever more informational history she had been assigned. She crosses her arms and looks moodily towards her teacher.

"Because only one of you is going to be a part of Snoweldon's political face when you grow up. He's a Dragon Sage. No one's going to judge Snoweldon by whether or not he knows about the Bithrock Revolt or Dimming Plague," Thoedore remarks dryly.

Cecily huffs but seems at least content with that answer.

"Now, I do believe that's class, and if you're late for your magic lesson again, Miss Elizabeth will be having words with me," Theodore chuckles weakly but does appear genuinely afraid of whoever this Elizabeth is.

Cecily breaks out into a grin that doesn't dim even as the historian continues with her homework.

"We'll pick back up next time with what we should have covered today. For homework, please write your own summary of history from the Origin People through to the end of the Dark Ages."

Cecily immediately begins stuffing her writing material back into her bag haphazardly. The little lizard takes a look, but it doesn't seem as if she's written a whole lot; it seems catching him up took most of the lesson.

"Thank you for the lesson, Maester Theodore," Cecily chirps happily.

She grabs the infant reptile from his seat atop the books and heads for the door.

"You're welcome, Milady. However, do try to make your homework legible this time around, hmmm?" the old man prods at his student before Cecily makes her escape.

The door closes behind them with a soft thud as Cecily carries him back into the hall.

Magic is apparently taught in an exterior building along the west side of the fortress. After leaving her history lesson, Cecily hurries down the hall and out a set of large, dark wooden doors to a courtyard. Unlike the garden or the horse's paddock, this area of the fort isn't clearly used for anything in particular. Instead, the sweet scent of dew and the sight of a gravel path cutting through unkempt grass greets him as he is carried outside.

Cecily heads towards a round, brick building that stands near a few fir trees. When she reaches it, she knocks firmly, using the heavy iron door knocker. After a moment of silence, the door opens to reveal the young mage from the knightly expedition the dragon had hitched a ride with. Wasn't his name Tain or Tan or something?

"Greetings, Lady Cecily. Miss Eliza is waiting for you in the sky room," Tain-something-or-another actually smiles as he greets Cecily and ushers her inside. The man then leaves them to their own devices.

Now, the little dragon looks around in awe at the interior of the building. The exterior had been boring gray

Reborn as a Defective Drake: Snoweldon's Dragon

stone bricks, with a few lanterns hung in the surrounding fir trees. But inside the mage's tower tells an entirely different story. The stone bricks are still there, but the light comes in the form of softly glowing orbs that float about the room. One shifts past him, and he darts a paw out to poke it. Soft, warm fluff greets his claws before the orb is floating swiftly away. Watching it feels almost like watching things float in zero gravity.

The room is circular, with a staircase following up or down the curve of the tower to either side. Beyond the staircases, a few tables and chairs have been arranged in the center of a circle of bookcases. Robed individuals wander around the room, picking up books or working on something over a bubbling cauldron. Colorful fabric hangs from the support beams, and richly colored rugs carpet the floor. He sees one mage asleep in a hammock, clearly having been in the middle or some research before dropping off. The poor mage's notes lay scattered across the floor.

He smells the scent of heady incense, and somehow, he can hear a lute playing in the distance, though he's sure no one here is actually playing an instrument. Clearly, this room has been specifically designed to provide comfort to its occupants.

Cecily doesn't pause here though. Instead, she turns promptly to begin ascending the stairs. After passing the first floor, the path is lit by stationary torches, and only a long passageway with doors greets the two. Oddly enough, the hall lacks windows, despite being on the exterior of the building.

Cecily continues down the hall without pause and then up the flight of steps at the end of it. This time, the room isn't lit very well at all. Instead, a domed ceiling appears to have a few dimly lit starry constellations that give the room some shadows and shapes. Under its faint light, the little dragon can just make out a round table and chairs in the center of the room. Three figures have gathered around it, with one thin one seated at it.

"Miss Eliza, I'm here for my lesson," Cecily greets the thin figure respectfully.

Turning, the figure reveals an impression of sharp cheekbones and a thin nose.

"Ah, hello Lady Cecily," a woman's voice greets before speaking to her companions. "Continue maintaining your scrying. We don't want to be caught unaware." Then, to Cecily, "We'll be practicing in the second basement today. I want to work with you on your control again."

The woman stands and all the little dragon can see of her is a thin, bone-like form. Then, she moves swiftly past them, the sound of heavy heels echoing off the wooden floorboards. Cecily turns and almost has to run to keep up; the little dragon can feel the quick movement of her legs. The woman's stride must be pretty long, as she's already entering the well-lit second floor by the time Cecily catches up.

In the light, he can see a long braid of black hair sweeping from side to side where it peeks out from under a long, red veil. The women's robes are a vibrant red, trimmed with gold. It's a marked difference from the other mages who wear black or purple robes. She leads Cecily down to the first floor and then down past the first basement room; a wide open padded area.

The next basement floor she leads them to is the same, a circular padded area with a few buckets of sand and water scattered about. Like the second floor, this room is also lit by wall mounted torches.

Stepping into the center of the room, the woman finally turns around. The firebreather takes in her face and can only find one word to describe it: sharp. She has a knife sharp nose, thin brows, and angular lips that should be beautiful, but are somehow triggering his need to run instead. Her eyes burn a dangerous yellow-hazel mix, he feels as though he's being watched by some sort of predator when she glances his way.

"Hello, Sage." She states her greeting like a formal letter: brief and to the point. "I am Elizabeth Vancs. I'm Cecily's magic instructor, and now, yours as well. I don't expect you to perform magic; I know that Sages are not capable of much of it. However, you will follow along with Cecily's lesson and learn the theory at least."

Despite the harshness of her words, the woman's tone remains painfully bland. She's addressing him, but she's not invested in him any more than she must to speak to him. It's a little whiplash-inducing after Historian Theodore's blatant awe and fascination. Elizabeth Vancs truly couldn't care less about him.

Not knowing what else to do, he chirps an affirmative. He'll learn. He's not sure why he wouldn't be able to perform magic. Was it due to his skin reflecting the magic? But he's still pretty excited to learn about magic. And...he's still going to at least try to perform magic. He *has* to, on his honor as a nerd! Or, former nerd. There are definitely no online MMORPGs in this world.

"Now, as you know Cecily, mana comes from the world around you and exists primarily in the secondary plane of existence. It exists naturally in all living things, but only the

Reborn as a Defective Drake: Snoweldon's Dragon

secondary plane contains an unlimited amount of mana. To perform the phenomena that we call magic, practitioners tap into that secondary plane's mana and manipulate it to create effects within our own plane. We channel the mana into our plane by using our bodies as conduits and then creating magic by manipulating it through a foci. We can use a foci to shorten incantations because foci have inherent magical properties to boost the power of the caster. Well-crafted foci will have mathematical structures inscribed into the foci to help with control and direction. However, to get to the foci, mana must pass through the caster's body. That's why you must remember, Cecily, to flirt with magic is to flirt with danger. A loss of control can result in a loss of an internal organ," Elizabeth instructs firmly.

She pins Cecily beneath her hawk-like gaze.

"Now, we'll be starting with crystallizing water today and moving along with your ice exercises. Try to focus on control and proper casting technique." Elizabeth moves over to a bucket of water.

Cecily sets down her bag with one arm and deposits him on a bench with the other.

"Stay here, okay? Don't get underfoot," she warns him.

Then, she roots through her bag for a moment before coming out with an honest-to-goodness magic wand. It's an actual magic wand. The little former-human just oggles it for a minute, unable to look away. It's dark wood, about as long as

Reborn as a Defective Drake: Snoweldon's Dragon

Cecily's forearm, and it has a red, oval-shaped stone at the tip. Faint light from within the gem belies the wand's magical nature. By the time he's done looking at it, Cecily has walked back to Elizabeth.

"Are you ready?" Elizabeth asks her student.

"Yes, teacher."

"Then begin. Gather and then freeze some of this water," Elizabeth commands. Cecily doesn't reply after that; she just points her wand at the bucket of water between the two of them. The light inside the gem brightens before a glob of water rises from the bucket. The little dragon watches with baited breath as the water floats midair. He can see that Cecily's control isn't perfect; droplets of water drip down from it and back into the bucket. But, the girl still manages to pull a fist-sized globe of water from the bucket without using anything more than a stick and her will.

It's incredible, being in the presence of actual magic. Butterflies flutter in his chest, and he can't bring himself to look away. Then Cecily furrows her brown in concentration, and a glowing circle appears at the tip of her wand. It's only present for a split second, but he can make out the red snowflake in the center before it fades with a cracking noise.

Cecily relaxes and reaches out her hand to pluck a fully-frozen orb from the air. Cool condensation creates white wisps around the orb, but she holds it out to her teacher without hesitation. The older mage plucks it from Cecily's hands and peers at it for a minute before nodding.

"It's solid. However, you still need to work on controlling all of the water you pull. Do the exercise again, but focus on keeping all of the water this time. Remember to wrap the mana you're controlling fully around the water, as if you're cupping it in your hands."

"Yes, teacher." Cecily turns back to the water bucket and once more points her wand at it.

Again, a globe of water gathers and ascends into the air. Again, however, water droplets fall from Cecily's water globe back into the bucket. With a huff, Cecily freezes what she still has floating with a crackle of angry ice. Pulling it from the air with her free hand, Cecily's already holding another water glob by the time she's set down the frozen one.

This one also drips. Cecily freezes it with a swift cascade of glittering ice. Then, she goes on to the next one. And the next. And the next. Truthfully, the little dragon can see that Cecily is improving with each try, but he's getting bored of sitting and watching her freeze the same thing over and over again. It may be magic, but the minutes have stretched long over it, and he's tired of doing nothing.

Sighing, he shifts a little and turns to look around the room. Some interesting staves and rods rest against the walls, but apart from a few buckets, benches and the aforementioned wooden tools, the room remains bare. He's about to give

Reborn as a Defective Drake: Snoweldon's Dragon

another sigh when a burst of color lights his vision in the space between blinks. Jerking about, he looks around but only sees the same underground training room. The little dragon tilts his head. What? He peers back toward Cecily and Elizabeth. He doesn't see anything that would cause any colors, and Cecily's still just freezing water. He blinks and feels the layers of his eyelids slide over his eye. However, in between eyelids, he manages to catch a glimpse of bright red and shimmering blue.

Freezing, he blinks again and is greeted with the same shades as he's blinking. Oh! He had realized after he'd hatched that he had more than one eyelid. He'd thought that it was to help him keep his eyes clean or help with swimming, but now it appeared as if there was a second purpose to it. Was it heat vision, like snakes do with their tongues? But his eyes aren't his tongue and that really doesn't make any sense at all...

He cocks his head to the side and slowly lowers his eyelids. A clear film seems to pass over his vision first, and he watches in awe as a red aura curls from Cecily's heart down to her wand. Then his actual, non-transparent eyelids slide shut. Opening his eyes, the Sage is just in time to see Cecily freeze another globe of water. Focusing hard on the sensation of the transparent eyelids shifting across his eyes, he blinks several times in an effort of pulling just the transparent eyelid down over his pupils. He wonders if it's something he's capable of— like, does the muscle for one eyelid control them both? But just when he's about to give up, he finally manages to get the cool shift of texture and pressure that's only just barely there.

And then, his world lights up in colors. Baleful orange, fragrant yellow, and rippling blue flare into being before him. It takes a moment of wide eyed staring to comprehend the dull gray sigils covering the walls, the gleaming yellow sparks littered on many of the magical tools, and the structured blue lines that overlay Elizabeth's form. Orange sparks waft from Cecily's wand and the heart red he'd seen earlier pools just above her belly button. When she goes to freeze another glob of water, he watches, transfixed, as the red spirals from her center. It passes up on some unseen passageway and then back down her arm to her wand. Once there, it vanishes within the dark wood before popping back into being at the tip of the wand's gem.

Except now it's been woven into a circle with numbers on the outside and a snowflake on the inside. The circle hits and collapses around the globe of water, freezing it over solid. At that point, the little dragon blinks and finds himself looking at a normal room again. The now-frozen orb is handed over to Elizabeth before Cecily starts another round of freezing water into ice balls.

In the meantime, the dragon takes a minute to just think over what he had just experienced. Now that he's able to see the colors moving in tandem with the rest of the world, he has a pretty good idea of what his extra eyelid does. It lets him see mana before it becomes magic. He's not sure if it lets him see into that secondary plane of infinite mana, since the light he saw didn't look very infinite. But he does know that he's at least seeing mana in transition from the secondary plane into magic.

Seeing it go from Cecily into her wand was interesting. It reminded him of coding. In order for a programmer to write code that the computer understands, the program has to be translated into binary code. Similarly, it seems that magic needs something it understands and that when Cecily runs her magic through her wand, she's translating her will and power into something that can actually be carried out. It's fascinating that something from modern Earth could be applicable to magic. Still, there's so much more to see!

He closes his second eyelids again and glances around. The walls are lit with soft gray magic that looks kind of old. It's shaped like someone decided to write entire paragraphs in hieroglyphic script, though he doesn't think these are Egyptian hieroglyphs.

Ideograms, yes. Egyptian, no.

Peering at it, he's intrigued to notice some worn out spaces on the paragraphs. It's like whatever was written there was washed away by something. With how old it was, and with Cecily's history lesson in mind, he wonders if these are the runes the old historian had been looking for. They certainly appear to be old enough, and if the runes are invisible to the

Reborn as a Defective Drake: Snoweldon's Dragon

naked eye, it would explain why no one had figured out how the castle provided heated water and heated floors.

Turning his eyes towards the staffs and other magical instruments lining the walls, he takes note of how the yellow light they give off tends to focus on either a crystal or the tip of the weapon. Just like Cecily's wand, most of these magical instruments have crystals socketed at the ends. Were these the focus gems he'd been hearing about all day? Even when he blinks and finds himself using his regular eyesight, the gems glow ominously.

Knowing of the vibrant magic they contain, he can see why they might glow even to the common eye. Turning back, he blinks his 'magic sense' on and watches Cecily hand over another frozen orb to her teacher. Then, a soft plume of red darts from that round, dense orb of mana within her to her wand. Unlike when she's working on freezing the water, this red mana stream is small and thin. Obviously, lifting the water takes much less power than freezing it. While freezing the water, the red mana strand is similarly absorbed by the wand before emerging again, transformed. Though, to his surprise, what comes from the other end of the wand is not a magic circle but a woven net of red strands with strange symbols embedded.

The net plummets into the bucket before pulling up a glob of water wrapped within its weave. Unfortunately for Cecily, her net has holes in it, and he watches with fascination as droplets of water leak from the net's holes and drip back to the bucket. Blinking back to normal vision, he watches as Cecily freezes this water glob as well. She's about to hand it to Elizabeth when the woman sighs.

"We've spent all but fifteen minutes of our time, Cecily. Please focus. This is a basic exercise." A hint of frustration creeps into the woman's voice.

Cecily winces but dutifully tries again. Once more, water splatters back into the bucket when she fails to hold it properly.

"I'm sorry, Eliza. I know I had this last time. I'm not sure what I'm doing wrong." Cecily says fretfully.

She casts her magic again, but she still can't stop a few droplets of water from escaping her hold. Though he's not looking through his magic eyelids, the little firebreather is sure that she's trying to use a net of magic to catch all of the water again. He watches her try again before moving forward. He's not sure what he can do to help, being voiceless and all, but he can't just sit here and watch her struggle. He knows what she's doing wrong. If can show her somehow, shouldn't he try?

He trots behind her and waits until she's just handed an icey sphere off to Elizabeth Vancs.

"Hey!" he squeaks as loudly as he can and paws gently at Cecily's socks.

"Little Sage?" Cecily turns around and peers down at him. "What's wrong? Are you hurt?"

Reborn as a Defective Drake: Snoweldon's Dragon

She reaches down and cups him within her hands. He nuzzles into the side instinctively before bringing his mind back to the matter at hand. It's a little embarrassing, what he's about to do. But he knows no other way to get his point across since he lacks a voice and opposable thumbs.

He points. And by points, he points in the way of all the good hunting dogs: the German pointer, the retriever, and even the bloodhound. He straightens his tail and spine, points his nose towards the bucket, and spreads his legs out. He lifts one front paw and raises his tail straight up into the air. Embarrassment burns at his cheeks in a heated blush, but he manages a passively stoic expression across his muzzle.

It does get his point across though.

"My water bucket?" Cecily looks back at the bucket. "Oh!" she exclaims.

Hope rises from his gullet.

"Are you thirsty?"

And the hope goes out with hiss and whine.

He shakes his head and points again, but this time to the wand she's got hooked into the sash on her waist. Finally, the girl catches on.

"My wand? Oh, you're talking about my casting," Cecily realizes.

She looks glumly down at him, and it takes him a minute to figure out the reason why. Cecily is insecure about her magic. She's clearly struggling with the control exercises her

Reborn as a Defective Drake: Snoweldon's Dragon

teacher has assigned her and doesn't like it when he points it out, similar to how he would feel if someone mentioned how poorly he wrote essays in college, Cecily doesn't like it when someone tells her she's not good at casting when she's clearly trying her best. Her teacher, Elizabeth Vancs, shifts closer, and he finds her observing him through steely eyes.

"Sages are recorded to be able to provide great insight to the magical process. Perhaps he is trying to offer you his aid in your casting," the woman speaks.

She doesn't take her gaze from the dragon's small form, even as Cecily replies.

"Really? But I thought Sages couldn't do magic?"

"They can, but only a little. Instead, they were good teachers and researchers into the development of the art of magic from mana. Apparently, their state of being lends them a specific advantage towards understanding mana before its use as magic. It could be that the Sage knows what you lack in your casting and is offering his knowledge," Elizabeth explains curtly.

"Really? You can help me do magic?" Cecily looks back down at the teacup sized dragon in her hands.

He blinks at the glimmer of want blooming in her eyes. Well, there's really only one answer he can give to that. He was planning to help her anyway, though he's not sure how to get his point across.

He nods a hesitant affirmative. Cecily smiles.

Reborn as a Defective Drake: Snoweldon's Dragon

"Oh thank you! I've been having so much trouble pulling water. I can pull other things like dirt or even furniture, but I just can't seem to pull up a whole glob of water without dropping it." The amount of brightness Cecily emits purely from that statement feels like it lights up the whole room.

Well, he definitely has to help her now. There's no way he won't after that level of unadulterated happiness.

"Now, what do I do?" Cecily asks him.

He blinks and gives a drawn out squeak. Then, he gestures to the bucket with his nose again. Shakily, he sits back on his haunches and puts his front paws together as if he's cupping water, but makes sure to leave visible gaps between his digits.

"Do you want me cast again?" the blonde girl asks.

He shakes his head and draws his claws farther apart.

"Is that... Are you trying to show me something with your claws?"

He nods and makes a scooping motion with his front legs. He then repeats it several times when Cecily doesn't seem to get it.

"Oh! Your claws...they're too far spread apart. Is that why I'm not catching all the water?" Cecily finally notices his claws.

When the firebreather nods, she frowns.

"But I don't know how to get the magic any tighter. I've woven as tightly as I can." She grits her teeth in frustration and sends a grumpy look towards the bucket.

He tilts his head and ponders what he can do to help her. Knowing what the problem was wasn't really helping. After all, her teacher had been telling her to cast a tighter hold on the water from the very beginning. Now the girl just had the confirmation of the issue at hand. It didn't actually help her fix it.

Giving a huff, he shifts about. Perhaps he could look at an up-close cast and give feedback on that? Maybe he'd be able to see something more now that he was closer. He looks at her and nudges her hand. She tilts her head, but waits till he points his nose towards the wand at her hip.

"Do you want me to cast it again?" The noble girl asks.

"Yup!" he chirps and nods his head.

She sighs, clearly still disappointed. Even so, she shifts him carefully to one hand and pulls out her wand with the other. When she takes her stance, he's situated near her body, pressed up against her stomach. The warmth of it feels good compared to the cool cellar air.

He feels her tense in preparation of casting, so he pulls his magic eyelids down. To his shock a greater warmth emanates from behind him, and he looks back to see that red core of mana within Cecily. Somehow, he can't just see the magic, he can also feel it as it radiates out and reflects off his skin. Obviously, he has to be close to someone while they're casting magic to do this, but it's no less an intriguing discovery for it. The warmth seeping from Cecily resonates with him in a gentle song of harmonious notes. Something in between his heart and his lungs heats up.

Red trickles of mana flow through invisible veins from her core to her arm and down to her fingers. Being this close, he can feel the way Cecily's own metaphysical being tugs and manipulates the strands even before they hit the wand. Yet, he can see and feel where the girl is going wrong. She's trying to weave a basket but lacks the proper skill to weave a waterproof basket. Learning to weave a proper basket would likely take months.

Luckily, he knows a shortcut. Back on Earth, people rarely used baskets to hold things and certainly not water. Instead, they used plastics, a substance created through gathering natural materials like plants and gas, refining them, treating them with high heat, and varying the amounts of what comes out to create different kinds of plastic. He's not certain of just how malleable magic is, but if it can be woven into a basket, then surely it can be molded like pottery or polymers.

Instinctively, he places a paw on her stomach and feels the energy there. It's not his, but he can feel it and therefore interact with it. This he knows instinctively, like opening his wings to glide or running from his older siblings when they wanted to kill and eat him. All it takes is a mental twist, an

Reborn as a Defective Drake: Snoweldon's Dragon

image of heat and perhaps an entirely fictitious thought of a mixing bowl. Plastic isn't really made in a mixing bowl, but it suits his purposes to imagine it. He carefully shifts Cecily's magic to contain instructions for making a bowl instead of a net before releasing it to her wand. The instructions feel clumsy, as he's relying entirely on will and a mental image to direct Cecily's magic. However, from what he's seen, Cecily does the same when she directs her own magic. It only feels clunky to him because he's used to coding complex, specific instructions to computers. With a mental nod to himself, the dragon releases the mana to the wand. From there, the runes on the wand translate his instructions into the spell.

Softly glowing sigils form in a circle around the bucket. A flood of obedient cherry red pools at the center, within the bucket. For a moment he's worried since a ball of water doesn't immediately rise. Luckily, his worry turns out to be unfounded as a red tinted globe of water rises smoothly into the air. This time when Cecily holds it up, no water escapes her hold.

With a deep breath, the girl freezes the globe and plucks it from the air. Blinking, the little dragon returns his sight to normal just in time for Cecily to clutch him close to her collar.

"Little Sage! You did it, you did it!" the girl cries excitedly.

Next to him, the frozen ice ball is also raised to her collar in her bid to hug him close. Its frigid surface causes him to let out a squeak of displeasure, and he shrinks away from it. Thankfully, Cecily's strict teacher comes to his rescue.

"Cecily. Enough. What has he done? Explain this." Again, the woman's words are said without tact, but the emotionless voice betrays no anger or negative emotion. The woman's mannerisms remind the dragon uncomfortably of a doll.

Elizabeth just doesn't seem to care overly much about how she talks. Cecily lowers her hands, moving the frozen water globe away from him. He sighs in relief and curls around himself, still feeling cold.

"He messed with the magic inside of me, and when I went to cast it, it came out differently. It's like...he melted it, and I was able to shape it using my wand."

"He was able to control the mana while you channeled it through your body?" Elizabeth frowns and seems a little unnerved. "What a disturbing ability..." she murmurs quietly.

Most likely, she had intended that part to herself since the little dragon could only barely hear it. He straightens and thinks over what he had done. True, messing with someone's mana while it was still in their body would likely seem very invasive to most people. But as he glances up at Cecily's continued smiling, it doesn't appear to bother Cecily much. Perhaps it would bother older mages because the younger mages weren't as used to magic? Technically, the mana they channeled through their bodies was foriegn as well; it was just something they likely became used to.

Reborn as a Defective Drake: Snoweldon's Dragon

"Yes, isn't that amazing? He could see what I was doing wrong and knew just how to fix it. And now I know how to fix it too! Watch!" Cecily's excitement covers her teacher's reticence like a palpable layer of fluffy joy.

She sets him down at her feet alongside the frozen orb in favor of grabbing her wand. Within moments, she's holding another perfectly frozen ball. She's copied his technique perfectly to shape her mana into a malleable substance rather than ropes. Her teacher's eyes widen briefly before returning to their normal width.

"Well done. Continue this for the rest of the lesson to make sure it sticks."

"Yes, teacher," Cecily aquisces.

She pouts a little, clearly ready to move on from doing the same thing over and over again. Meanwhile, Elizabeth watches the dragon with dark eyes.

After the magic lesson, Cecily hurries to grab some food from the kitchens. Unlike what the little dragon had expected of a noble's fortress, it seems that lunch is an informal affair. Unimportant people fetch lunch from the kitchens, or servants send out carts with food for large groups of people. Meanwhile, nobles or people with important jobs have personal meals fetched for them by servants.

Cecily likely could have had her meal fetched by the servants, but she just grabs a meal basket from the kitchen and continues onward. When they head into the kitchen, Cecily is careful to situate the little dragon on her shoulder, partially hidden by her braids. Somehow, people don't seem to notice him on her shoulder, but perhaps, that's just his white scales blending into her white collar. At any rate, Cecily zips in and out as if the hounds of hell nip at her feet. He has just enough time to smell freshly baked bread and heady seasoning before she's already leaving the kitchen behind her with her meal hung on her arm. He watches as immaculate stone halls pass by.

Again, Cecily passes through the great hall she had passed through earlier. She waves to her father, still seated at his chair and working though a basket of food that has been delivered to his side. The number of finely dressed people around the man have grown, and there are several other clusters of people eating their lunch about the hall.

Cecily bypasses them to head down a smaller corridor though. Like the others, this corridor is lit by torches; but at the end of it; a glass window set in a wooden door lets in the noonday sun. This passageway seems smaller than most, only a few feet wide; so the little reptile wonders if it's a servant passage.

Either way, when Cecily opens the door, the sunlight blinds him. On this clear day, the sun beams down like a spotlight upon the whole world. He finds himself blinking both eyelids several times as he adjusts to it. Looking around, he spots the fountain Cecily had dumped him in last night. Since Cecily has left the building at a different angle, it's not directly in their path. Instead, a flower ringed courtyard lies ahead. Towering fir trees provide shade to a circular patch of ground devoid of grass. The same obsidian that lines the rest of the outdoor walkways carves out a rough circle beneath the trees.

It is to this area that Cecily carries him. When they draw closer, he sees that there's already someone there, waiting.

"Good day, Lady Cecily," the man greets as he steps from his place against a tall fir.

Reborn as a Defective Drake: Snoweldon's Dragon

His movement into the light reveals curly, brown hair and odd amethyst-colored eyes. He wears his hair long, in a low ponytail that reaches the top of his leather breeches. He's donned a blue tunic, and seems lightly dressed compared to the other people the Sage has had the chance to see. The man wears no overcoat or vest, though what he does have is embroidered finely at the hems. A silver rapier rests at his waist, and even his stance reveals a level of grace, as the man rests on the balls of his feet. He's physically fit too, not overly so like some of the body builders that make onlookers feel awkward, but with a lithe grace that can be attributed to a healthy workout routine.

"Maester Dorian, greetings!" Cecily hurries forward as she greets her teacher.

This man is Cecily's dance instructor, the little dragon remembers. Cecily had spoken of enjoying his lessons because he also taught her what sounded like parkour mixed with self-defense.

Cecily sets the basket down on a nearby bench and gently lifts the dragon from her shoulder to set him beside the basket.

"This is my dance instructor, Little Sage." Cecily introduces the man to him. "Maester Dorian, this the Sage. Father said he is to attend all of my lessons with me."

"I see," Dorian says and leans down to get a closer look at the infant beast. He stops about a foot away. "And he's intelligent? He can understand us and everything?"

The man positions himself this way and that, trying to take in the small dragon's appearance fully. The dragonet wrinkles his nose and leans back. He doesn't appreciate being stared at. More than that, Dorian's eyes gleam dangerously. Combined with Dorian's obvious capability, the little dragon does not want to be the object of the swordsman's fascination. He has the feeling being so would be bad for his continued good health.

"Yes! He helped me in my magic lessons today. Eliza says that Sages are more in tune with mana and the world than anything else," Cecily announces proudly. She runs a careful two fingers down his spine.

"How interesting. Does he have a name?" A new voice asks.

The dragon looks over to see a blonde youth enter the courtyard. From the state of his brown breeches and red vest, he appears to be another servant here in the fort. The dragon would have continued trying to pierce the young man together, but he's distracted by Cecily's outraged cry.

"Sanders, no!" The girl gasps out in horror. "You can't name a monster! It's bad!"

She snatches the dragon off the bench fearfully and even goes so far as to cover his ears. Meanwhile, he can't help the

Reborn as a Defective Drake: Snoweldon's Dragon

shocked shriek that pours from his snout. He blinks dizzily up at the horrified visage of the noble child. What was wrong with naming him? Or, perhaps the bigger question is why doesn't he have a name? As a human, his name had been Isaac. Shouldn't he have just used that name for himself? It's his name. His mother gave it to him.

Except... he can't. There's something wrong; he realizes he fails to use his own name, even in his thoughts. He can't use his name. He doesn't know why. He just knows that he's not Isaac anymore. In fact, he's not anyone. Right now, he's just a dragon. And that's...weird. To have those facts pressed into his head like physical weight, to pull at his thoughts and feelings like some sort of anchor? It's a bizarre sensation, but he can't shake it either. He's not Isaac. He's a dragon, and he will continue to be until he's given a name. He's not sure why, just that something important in him doesn't have something, feels empty and cold, and it won't be filled until he's given a name. It's something that only someone else can give him because he's lacking...something.

He's lacking something. The thought sits on his mind just long enough for sorrow to creep in beside the fear of being nameless. Before he can seep too deeply into either negative emotion, Cecily's voice brings him back to the present.

"Naming a monster links the name giver and monster for life, Sanders. It casts a binding contract between the monster and the person who names them, enabling the

Reborn as a Defective Drake: Snoweldon's Dragon

monster to gain access to that person's mana and vice-versa. It's extremely dangerous and hasn't been done in hundreds of years." Cecily sounds incredibly like an adult, even with the childish lilt her voice still carries.

Yet, her somber tone pulls at her future self, of when Cecily will be grown, a powerful mage and noble woman in her own right. He blinks owlishly at her. He hadn't thought she could be so mature.

"So, he won't ever have a name? Then what do you call him?" Sanders asks.

The teenager has taken a step back and is appraising the dragon with significantly more caution now. It seems that he hadn't really considered the infant reptile to be too dangerous before, or maybe he'd just been temporarily overcome with excitement. At any rate, Sander's excitement has faded. Instead, the teen examines the dragon curiously but carefully and doesn't approach.

"I've been calling him Little Sage. It's a title in the same way 'dragon' would be, but it's more personal, so I think he likes it more," Cecily explains. Again, she drags two gentle fingers down his spine. He closes his eyes at the pleasant sensation.

"That's a good idea, Lady Cecily. It'll keep commoners from naming him by accident, too, if he's ever around them," Dorian comments from the side. The little dragon looks up at him.

Reborn as a Defective Drake: Snoweldon's Dragon

His eyes haven't left the little dragon's form, but something about him has relaxed a little. A tenseness in his shoulders maybe?

"Well, it shouldn't be too much of a problem for commoners actually," Cecily contradicts. "Naming monsters requires a lot of mana, and most commoners can't pull that much even when trained. It's just those with noble blood that have to worry."

The little dragon blinks. He won't be named, and he's not sure if he likes that option or not. Being connected so intimately to someone sounds horrible, but being without a name isn't that great either. He misses having a name, and now that he's aware of it, that empty space inside of him burns for something. He's missing a piece of his puzzle, and he knows he won't feel any better until that piece has been slotted into place.

"I see." Dorian nods to himself before continuing. "Now, we've already wasted some of our time, so hurry and eat milady. We'll be dancing today since you lack proper attire for other physical activities."

Cecily nods and sets the Little Sage back down on the bench beside her to begin unboxing the basket she'd grabbed from the kitchen. As soon as she takes the lid off, he's met with the tantalizing aroma of smoked ham and mashed potatoes. The basket rises a few inches above his head, so he scampers forward and rears up on his hind legs. With his front paws on the edge, he can just see some sliced cheese next to some bread and ham. The mashed potatoes must be out of his range of sight, behind the basket weave he's leaning over.

"Are you hungry, Little Sage?" Cecily asks him.

"Yes!" He chirps excitedly.

He flutters his wings and wags his tail, but the backdraft sends him tumbling backwards with a sharp shriek. The landing on the bench doesn't hurt since he hadn't fallen too far, but it does surprise him a bit. He'd almost forgotten about his wings throughout the day since Cecily had been carrying him all day. Now that he's flat on his back because of them, it's like they pop back up on his radar. Can he fly? He was able to glide away from the peaks he hatched from, but that's entirely different than winning against gravity. Cecily interrupts him from any further pondering though.

"Careful, Little Sage." She carefully picks him up and sets him upright.

He chirps in agreement and starts drooling when he sees her lifting out some ham for him to eat. It smells so good! As soon as she sets it on the bench beside him, he chomps down. All of the new things he'd learned and experienced that morning had kept him distracted, but now that food is in front of his face again, a roaring hunger has awakened in his stomach.

He chews and swallows only to take another bite as quickly as he can. Within what feels like moments the entire slice of meat has been devoured, but his stomach still feels empty. Turning to Cecily, he whines pitifully. She takes a bite of a ham and cheese sandwich, but does pass over another chunk of sweet ham. He tears into it as swiftly as he did the first one. He swallows down each bite so quickly that he barely even has time to taste it. Luckily, this second slice of ham seems to do the trick, or at least, he's not ravenously hungry anymore.

Glancing up, he notices that Cecily's not seated on the bench beside him anymore. He'd been so busy eating the whole world had sort of faded away. Which is probably due to being a baby dragon with a baby dragon's appetite, but still. He needs to have more awareness than that. Turning, he spots Cecily standing in the middle of the courtyard with Dorian, just as the sound of a flute pierces the air. Immediately, Dorian holds out his hand to Cecily and begins leading her in a dance. The little dragon can't tell what kind of dance it is, as he's never been interested in dancing himself, but he can tell it's a slow dance. Cecily has one small arm awkwardly placed halfway up Dorian's chest due to the man's height. Somehow, Dorian manages to not look awkward as he bends over slightly to lead Cecily.

Looking for the flute player, the little dragon is a little surprised to see Sanders playing a wooden flute. Sanders hadn't really seemed the type to play a flute, yet there he is. If the peaceful look on his face is any sign, the kid enjoys playing the flute, too. With a satisfied nod, the little lizard turns back to watch Cecily spin around the courtyard. His lunch sits heavy in his belly, and the sun peeks through the fir trees to land just across his shoulder blades. He yawns and settles himself down on his stomach. He's getting...kinda...sleepy.

… … … … …

Warm fingers tickling over his back and wings rouse him. Blinking, he's surprised by the orange color that's seeped into his surroundings. Hadn't it only just been midday?

"Little Sage, It's time to wake up." Cecily's voice drifts down from above.

He looks up into her cerulean eyes, and she smiles back down at him. The evening sun turns her hair orange in the places it can reach while the rest seeps a darkening purple shadow. He yawns but perks up when she lifts him to rest on her shoulder. He squeezes his claws for a better grip and settles himself just below her ear. Looking about, he can see that he's been sleeping for at least a few hours. The sun has tread slowly across the sky and now paints the garden in hues of gold, red, and orange.

Cecily's the only one left in the garden. He doesn't see either Sanders or Dorian, so they must have already finished the dance lesson. Considering the placement of the sun, it would be alarming if they were still dancing.

Cecily carries him inside and down the narrow passageway again. The torches still provide light to the passageway, but the lack of sunlight from either end of the hall causes a definite change in atmosphere. He curls closer to Cecily's neck. Without natural lighting, the fortress has become ominous and shadowed. Luckily, Cecily heads into a large and well lit hall. Ahead of her, a long, red tinted table provides the centerpiece to a pristine dining room. Light streams from a multi-tier, candle lit chandelier hanging above. Tapestries and stained glass windows line the halls, with the fading light turning them to shimmering autumn colors

The table's occupants attract most of the little Sage's attention though. At the head, an older, gray-haired man sits. His skin shows his age in wrinkles while his clothes serve as evidence to a recent weight loss with their bagginess on his thin frame. To his right, the Lord of Snoweldon chats with him. From here, the little dragon can just hear their conversation.

"How many have fallen ill in the town?" The elder Snoweldon asks.

"Over five hundred that have been reported. The Captain of the Guard thinks that there may be more in the slums that haven't been reported or who have already passed unnoticed. In the fortress, most of our cooking staff, the maids and cleaning staff, and even many of our soldiers have fallen ill.

Reborn as a Defective Drake: Snoweldon's Dragon

This is becoming serious." The Lord of Snoweldon furrows his brow in concern.

There's a tenseness to his shoulders that wasn't there the night before, too. Instinctively, the little dragon can tell that there must be something very, very wrong for a man so level-headed to be so easily showing his upset.

"And it happened so quickly too. Just yesterday, the first reports of illness came in. Now the fortress is running on our reserve workforce."

To the elderly man's left, a young man enters the conversation. The dragon can tell from his voice that this is Cecily's oldest brother: Calvin. Like his father, the young man sports a dark head of hair, a sharp nose, strong jaw, and glimmering blue eyes like Cecily.

"I don't like this. It's too sudden," the only woman at the table, Selina, comments.

She sits beside her husband. Her blonde hair hangs long from her half-up ponytail. Long braids ring her face with links of gold, and when she moves, the chains and precious stones in her hair jingle. Instead of an apron, she wears what the dragon had at first expected of a medieval noblewomen. Her dress consists of a white flowing underdress and a dark blue overdress tied together in the front with strings. It gives the appearance of a dress with several layers, but after seeing Cecily's many layers, he can tell that it's two different dresses. The overdress clings to the woman's body down to the hips

Reborn as a Defective Drake: Snoweldon's Dragon

where it flows out.Her sleeves are similarly tight up to the elbow before becoming the long, flowy sleeves seen in fantasy video games.

There's an empty chair next to her, presumably Cecily's, with two plates of food set in front. Across from her, a younger boy, probably Conner, chews slowly on whatever he'd previously stuck in his mouth. Like his elder brother and father, he also has dark hair, but his eyes gleam a dull green. Something feels off, though. The child seems exhausted, and there appears to be a red flush to his cheeks. Worry creeps into the dragon's gut as Cecily takes a seat across from Conner. Something is amiss. There's no way an illness could spread so quickly. From the way the Snoweldon adults speak, the situation is quickly becoming dire. And, if what his gut is telling him is true, the problem at hand may have already spread to this very table.

"Indeed, it is. A day and a half, and already we've come to this. This can't be any ordinary illness." The old man at the head of the table confirms what the others likely hadn't wanted to say. Or, in his case, *couldn't* say.

Something flickers on the edges of the Little Sage's vision.

"Has it really become so bad?" Cecily pipes up.

She sets him on the table, where a second plate has been set up for him. Some fish has been cut into little chunks, and unlike the others', his has been served raw. Selina and

Calvin look him over, but Calvin quickly returns his attention to the papers laid before him. Selina, unfortunately, does not look away. Rather, she stares at the lizard in disgust. It's only after Cecily moves slightly in between them that the woman looks back towards her husband. Somehow, he feels like this dinner would have been much more uncomfortable for him had something much more dire not been at the forefront of everyone's minds.

"I'm afraid so. Yesterday, we received the first reports of maids or kitchen staff becoming ill within the fort, and now, our clinics in the city are nearly full of the afflicted." Conwell turns towards his children with a worried eye. "If you feel ill, even a little, I want you to go straight to the healers, okay? This illness is very dangerous."

"Yes, father," all three children echo their father.

"If it's unnatural, then what's causing it?" Conner asks.

He's frowning down at his food as if his radishes hold the antidote captive. He blinks sleepily, as though tired. The worry curled in the dragonet's gut claws at his insides.

"I'm not sure. If it's affecting both the fort and the city, then we must both come into contact with it regularly, so that rules out a foriegn illness. If someone came in with it, the city would have had more cases first, and then it would have spread. We've had no diplomats either. Everyone passing through the gates has been checked, and no one unique or from far away came through." Conwell drums his fingers on the table

Reborn as a Defective Drake: Snoweldon's Dragon

in thought while he answers his son's question. "We also have spells that check for foriegn contaminants at our gates. There is always the chance it came in with smuggled goods, but if that were the case we would have seen it impact the slums in a big way before it ever affected the fortress or inner markets."

Meanwhile, Cecily begins to eat her food. The little dragon takes that as his cue to begin filling his belly as well.

"It can't be our food supply either," Calvin murmurs. He, too, looks at his plate in thought. "The fort's food is always checked extensively for poisons, and it comes directly from a farmer we contract with. Also, from the reports, people got sick in town at about the same time as our first cases were reported. If it were from the food, it'd be a gradual thing, as not everyone gets shipments at the same time and most certainly not from the same farm."

So not the food and not likely a foriegn pathogen? Just what was causing people to fall sick? And what were the symptoms anyway? Vomiting typically meant a food or water-related illness while coughing was a sign of a respiratory illness. Which, granted, didn't mean much, as fevers could cause vomiting, and one didn't need to have the strep cough to sneeze.

"It must be something we all use. Is there anything among the first few ill that linked them together?" the elder, still unnamed in the dragon's mind, asks with his crackling voice.

Reborn as a Defective Drake: Snoweldon's Dragon

Calvin bends over some sheets of parchment in front of him and hums.

"The first reported victims were primarily bakers, kitchen staff, the morning hearth tenders, and some of the night guard. All from different living quarters and backgrounds with different jobs."

"Different ages as well. Men and women." Conwell adds his two cents. "There doesn't seem to be anything connecting any of them."

"But father... don't they all get up early?" Cecily's voice splits the tension that had been mounting. "All of those people, they have to wake up early to go to work. The soldiers have to stand guard, someone has to gather wood and light the hearths, kitchen staff have to prep everyone's breakfast, and bakers have to wake really early to prepare the morning bread." The little dragon looks over at Cecily in surprise. She hadn't seemed to be taking part in the conversation any longer, and he had assumed she wasn't listening. It would appear she had been deep in thought all along.

"Cecily, you're right! The people who were affected first are all people who wake the earliest!" Calvin exclaims.

He hurriedly pours over the papers again, shifting through them with gusto.

"Yes, but that still doesn't tell us what's making them sick. We still need to find out what they touched so early in the morning that caused them to fall ill," Conwell murmurs.

Reborn as a Defective Drake: Snoweldon's Dragon

"Or ate. Maybe a pathogen was delivered to their food?"

"Too unpredictable. It's true something may have been smuggled into the city and that many of the servants do live in the servants' quarters, but the guards and some of the staff sleep and take their first meal elsewhere." Selina enters the conversation acerbically.

Her tone cuts through the air like a blade, and it's clear she's not happy with the situation. The woman leans over to pull Cecily against her side fretfully, running her fingers along Cecily's braids.

"What's the one thing they all have access to in the morning? We know they eat, but they can't have been poisoned for their breakfast, and they all work in different areas." Conwell asks. The nobles likely would have continued to seek out the cause of the illness, had a crash not sounded out from the other end of the table. The dragon whips his head around to stare at the now-vacant seat across from Cecily. The goblet of water rolls noisily across the table, and water has flooded over the table cloth on that side. Worry sings in the dragon's gut as he looks at the scene with wide eyes. He blinks and a putrid green flashes across his retinas. This time at least, he hates being proven right.

"Conner!" Selina shouts as she rushes around the table in a flurry of blue fabric.

Her husband follows not two steps behind her.

"Send for Healer Aguine!" The Snoweldon Lord orders one of the servants posted at the doors.

The young man bolts almost before Conwell stops talking, his footsteps sounding loudly down the corridor. Behind him, Cecily stands as well. Like her parents, she hurries around the end of the table to her brother. Following the others, the dragon scampers over to the other side of the table. He trips over a fork and ends up rolling to a stop in the water spilled by the cup. Blinking, he flinches at the haze of poisonous green that flashes across his vision. He sneezes and shakes his head. Luckily, the family doesn't notice.

"Conner, wake up!" Selina urges her son from the ground.

The little dragon peeks over the edge of the table to see the Snoweldon's youngest son lying limply in his mother's arms. Conwell places a hand over his child's brow and frowns.

"He's burning with fever. We've got to bring it down." Conwell follows his statement with cupping both hands.

Ice blooms within his palms, and he quickly presses it to Conner's forehead. So Cecily's father can use ice magic too? And without gathering water first, too.

"What's wrong with him?" Cecily asks. She approaches slowly from behind her mother. "He was fine just a minute ago."

Other than biting her lip, Cecily appears to be keeping a clear head. In comparison to Selina, who has started

Reborn as a Defective Drake: Snoweldon's Dragon

murmuring sweet nothings into her son's ear, she's taking this much better. Or perhaps, her youth merely protects her from acknowledging the worst that can happen?

Meanwhile, the baby lizard ponders her words. Conner had seemed kind of tired, but not about to collapse. Had there been something at the table that set this off? He peers at Conner's seat and plate, but he doesn't see anything amiss. The boy hadn't even really started eating; apparently, he disliked the fish and vegetables served. The only thing Conner had touched was the goblet of water...

"Father..." Calvin has stepped forward. "Is it... the sickness? Did he catch it?"

The young man eyes his brother with no little trepidation. Worry turns his brow into a mess of colliding angles, and his frown pulls at his cheeks. The little dragon pads back over to the water but keeps an ear tuned to the humans' conversation. He sniffs the water. It doesn't smell like any poison. It kind of smells like metal, but it likely came from metal piping or sat in a metal pitcher. Otherwise, it smells like ordinary water. He looks at the silver goblet. Doesn't poison turn silver different colors? He thinks he saw that on a movie once, but the gauntlet Conner used doesn't appear discolored.

"Most likely," Conwell confirms. "Stay back, Cecily. I don't want you catching it," he warns when Cecily takes another step forward.

Reborn as a Defective Drake: Snoweldon's Dragon

So, it might not be poison, but what could it be? The little dragon turns the problem over and over again in his mind. He blinks and is rewarded with a spasm of ugly green across his vision.

Oh.

He wants to roll his eyes.

Of course. Magic. Because what else would you use to poison people in a fantasy world?

"But Father," Cecily tries to argue.

He flicks his magic eyelids down and peers about. As he suspected, the water glows a dirty green. The magic within it gleams insidiously across the table. Some of it even lingers on his front legs and barrel chest from where he's tripped into it.

"No. You're a child. You'll catch it more easily if it's spread by contact."

There's a pause where Cecily shifts from foot to foot before she agrees in discontent. The Little Sage looks towards the other goblets and feels horror creep up his throat. The same green within Conner's goblet floats in the other goblets as well. Even the water pitcher in the center of the table gleams with that noxious light. All of their water tonight holds magic poison. If this is what's been causing people to fall ill, either someone has been very, very busy slipping it into cups... or the city's water source has been contaminated.

"Yes, Father."

Reborn as a Defective Drake: Snoweldon's Dragon

They were all intended to be poisoned. From the nobles down to the smallest beggar child; every person in the city had had their lives weighed and then slated for death. The water system has been compromised by a magical poison either intentionally or by mismanagement. That's why the first affected had been the first to wake for the day. They were the first exposed because they were the first to drink enough of the water to become ill. How many have been exposed by now? A whine escapes his throat as realization dawns on him.

It's been over twenty-four hours since the water system was compromised. Everyone in the city has been exposed. The only question remaining is how much exposure is needed to disable or kill the victims. A cup? Two cups? How much poison is needed to kill someone? Terror inches its way up his spine. He'd had water too. Would he get sick and die? How much poison water can a baby dragon drink without dying? Panic forces its way out of him in the form of several high pitched keens.

"Little Sage?" Cecil asks. She'd probably heard him whining, the dragon realizes. "Are you okay?"

She walks over and picks him up, running soothing fingers down his back. He looks up at her in despair. Has Cecily drunk enough of the poison to get sick yet? Are they all going to get sick and die without being able to do anything about it? His breaths come in quick, useless pants.

"Cecily! We're all going to die!" he whines piteously.

Reborn as a Defective Drake: Snoweldon's Dragon

He nuzzles into her belly for comfort.

"What's wrong with him?" Calvin asks. The young man approaches from the other side. "Is he scared?"

"It doesn't matter what's wrong with the creature! My baby's sick!" Selina cries out fretfully. "Conwell, look at Conner!" she demands distraughtfully when Conwell takes a step towards Cecily.

The Sage picks his head up and looks at the Snoweldons surrounding him. Then, he points at the water and whines. Cecily catches on quickly, having had a full day of charades with him.

She places him back on the table. His feet barely touch the ground before he's bounding over to the spilled water and goblet. As soon as he gets to the edge of the mess, he plops his butt down, throws his head back, and screams as loudly as he can. When he runs out of breath, he just inhales and starts screaming again. He's opening his mouth for the third time when a calloused hand covers his mouth.

"Alright, alright! You want our attention; you've got it," the eldest Snoweldon tells him in his crackly old voice. The old man leans over him like some kind of bony Batman and gives him a look reminiscent of the comic book hero. It cuts through his panic nicely enough.

The little dragon blinks and looks around. Oh, yes. He certainly has their attention. Even the white-robed newcomers have stopped to stare at him. Well. Time to get to it.

Reborn as a Defective Drake: Snoweldon's Dragon

Dipping a claw into the water, he holds it up to his face and makes exaggerated swallowing noises. Then, he rolls over and plays dead. This gets the point across fairly quickly.

"My baby's been poisoned?!" Selina gasps.

Calvin rubs his fingers through the water and brings it back to his nose to smell it.

"I don't smell anything," he admits with a frown. The young adult grabs the goblet and looks it over. "There's no residue here, either." He addresses the dragon. "Are you sure he was poisoned and isn't just sick?"

The Little Sage shakes his head in frustration.

These people!

Giving a little growl, he races across the table and knocks Cecily's water over. Then, he goes to the next goblet and repeats the process.

"Hey! Stop that!" Calvin shouts. The young man reaches to grab the dragon but gets bitten for his troubles instead. "Ouch!"

The Little Sage runs around the table, knocking each goblet over. Once the table has been successfully flooded, he headbutts the pitcher. It doesn't fall over, or even wobble, as it's still full of water. However, it does make a loud and very satisfying **'ding'** noise.

"It's the water! The water is making everyone sick!" Cecily gasps out.

Reborn as a Defective Drake: Snoweldon's Dragon

Finally! Someone gets it! he thinks to himself in exasperation. He croons exaggeratedly to make sure the other humans understand that Cecily has correctly deduced what he's trying to tell them.

Just how many goblets did he have to knock over to get the point across? Six?

"But that's not possible. All of Snoweldon uses the ancient irrigation system created by our ancestors. It's been hidden and locked away for years to keep it from being accessed or tampered with. No one's actually known where the source of it is for decades." Conwell shakes his head in disagreement.

"No, it makes sense." The elder Snoweldon looks at the water with a dark gleam. "If we don't know where it is, we won't be able to fix it. Someone's done their research on our most vulnerable points, entered into our most sacred of places..." He trails off and strokes his chin thoughtfully.

"But, if it's in the water, then that means everyone has already been exposed." A portly man comes forward.

He's dressed in white, clean robes with a yellow sash around his waist. Upon his head, he wears a round, flat hat with several different colored tassels falling behind him. Perhaps an indication of rank, like often found in graduation ceremonies of universities? The scent of bitter herbs wafts forward, and the dragon can spy a few strangely-colored bottles peeking from a brown satchel worn at the waist.

Reborn as a Defective Drake: Snoweldon's Dragon

"Healer Aguine," Conwell greets with relief written in the form of his sagging shoulders. "Conner...is he...?"

"He has caught the illness that's been going around, yes. However, you need not worry. Despite his fainting spell, he's quite stable. This illness is slow-working despite the difficulty we've found in treating it. I've checked him over; beyond being feverish, low on mana, and dehydrated, there's nothing actually amiss. Just as it has been for all of the others." Aguine gestures back to where some other white-robed humans were looking over Conner.

These people wear the same white robe ensemble that Aguin does, but their hats don't have as many ribbons. The other healers had at some point pulled the child away from Selina's grasp and now appear to be loading him into some kind of stretcher. In absence of her child, Selina runs her hands fretfully over her skirts. Her thin hands pinch and pull at the fabric in such a way that would surely insure it would not last long.

"So it's true, then. The illness isn't fatal?" Calvin asks. "The reports stated that no one had died, but so many are ill and unable to return to work."

He looks hopefully at his brother. Sadly, his optimistic expression doesn't last as Aguine begins speaking.

"No one has died in our clinics yet and we haven't found any bodies that can't be attributed to another ongoing health issue, Young Master. This disease targets the infirm and the

Reborn as a Defective Drake: Snoweldon's Dragon

elderly. So far we've been lucky enough to stabilize those worse affected so long as they reach our hospice doors. However, there are many worsening cases, and we haven't yet been able to cure or discourage the worst of the symptoms. If we don't find an antidote or something soon, we will be seeing healthy people die." The healer's voice shakes with apprehension, and his wrinkled face contorts itself in his anxiety.

From his countenance alone, the tension in the room thickens. If the healer most trusted by the Lord of Snoweldon believes the situation is dire, is the situation not dire indeed?

The little dragon whines to himself quietly. Luckily, Cecily quickly scoops him into her arms again. She runs her fingers down his spine. It feels pleasant to have something following the curves of his raised bumps, and he presses into her touch. After a few more strokes, he finds himself calming down from his earlier panic. Perhaps the movement releases endorphins similar to how children's bodies release endorphins when their backs are rubbed soothingly. But the baby dragon version, instead.

"Well, if it's in the water, can you find an antidote from there? And is it a slow acting poison or an illness?" Cecily asks.

She wrinkles her blond eyebrows at the puzzle. The dragon nods his head fretfully.

Many illnesses did come from contaminated water sources growing bacteria, but it could be a poisoned water source, too. It all depends on why people are actually sick. Are they ill from a bacteria in the water or from a toxin not meant to be ingested by humans? Maybe the body could sweat it out if they avoided drinking the water for a while? It does seem to take a certain amount to affect people, given that Cecily is still fine. The other nobles don't appear ill, either. Not everyone in the town or the castle had fallen ill yet, despite everyone having been exposed to it for over twenty-four hours.

"Due to how quickly it seemed to be spreading, I had assumed an illness. But with the knowledge that it came from our water system, it could very well be a slow acting poison that mimics being ill. And yes, knowing what is causing it can lead to a cure just as much as it can lead to avoiding any more cases." The healer looks meaningfully at Conwell.

Conwell startles, and between one blink and the next, he strides into action.

"Sylvan," Lord Snoweldon calls to one of the servants.

This man is well dressed in red breeches and a purple waist coat. He wears a weird, feathery hat atop his curly brown hair. Sylvan's long face reminds the dragon of a weasel, and his thin, focused gray eyes do nothing to disturb the image. Sylvan seems familiar, but it takes the dragon a minute to realize that Sylvan had been one of the attendants constantly following Lord Snoweldon around all day. A cooler version of a secretary maybe?

"Go and call the guard captains of each city district. Summon all of our remaining messengers as well. We'll be having an emergency meeting in the great hall."

While Conwell makes preparations to meet with his officers, Aguine steps forward and peers into the pitcher. Nodding to himself, he grabs a few of the goblets and sets them upright.

"Yes, Milord." Sylvan spares a moment for courtly manners before he's gone from the room.

The sharp clatter of his retreating heels echo loudly on the stone floor.

Servant sent, Conwell turns back to Aguine. The man has poured a small amount of water from the pitcher into each goblet now. From his satchel, he pulls several small, multicolored vials.

"How long until you know if you can find a cure? And are there any other preventative measures to be taken beyond putting the city on a 'no water' policy?"

A differently colored substance is dripped into each goblet. Aguine studies whatever resides in each goblet critically, occasionally stirring with a spoon. Whatever he finds must displease him, for he sets the last goblet down with a frown and a sigh.

"No, I don't believe so. The toxin only appears to react when ingested, as no one has reported any skin reactions. Rather, it causes the body to urinate more frequently and

Reborn as a Defective Drake: Snoweldon's Dragon

drains the mana supply. The body seems to react by becoming feverish, but it's the dehydration and the mana drain that's the biggest concern. It's also why no adult nobles have fallen ill yet; your kind tend to have higher mana reserves than most commoners. Now that I know what it's from, I believe the fever and the urination are the body trying to repel the toxin, as most toxins trigger either a sweat or immediate repulsion from the body. In this case, something in the water is draining mana and causing the body to reject the water once it gets to the kidneys. As for a cure... well, that depends."

"Depends on what?" Selina asks.

The poor woman looks overwrought with worry. The little dragon can't blame her. She's just seen one of her youngest babies collapse with an unknown illness or poison. He doesn't think he'd do much better in her place. As it is, the only thing keeping him from freaking out further is Cecily's reassuring hold on him.

"Whether or not I can find the toxin in the water. As you've said, it has no scent, and the water's not discolored. I'll be testing its purity, but some poisons can be purely magical and transparant against mundane techniques. The common indicators I carry with me haven't indicated any common causes." Here, the healer gestures to the goblets he'd been stirring and evaluating. "I'll likely need to seek out Madame Elizabeth if that's the case. She'll be able to provide illumination to any magical toxin or cause. Once I can actually

Reborn as a Defective Drake: Snoweldon's Dragon

see what I'm working with, I'll know better what to use to treat it. If it's an illness, I'll be able to find a cure to fight off the infection. If it's poison...I will need to have knowledge of it to know what to use as an antidote."

The room quiets after that. The implication of the words hold the room hostage for those who understand. The little dragon presses his head more firmly against Cecily's shirt. Even her finger running along the ridges down his spine doesn't comfort him nearly enough to shake the fear gripping his heart.

"What happens if you don't know the poison?" Cecily asks when the moment of silence becomes too much.

Young, smart, but not experienced, the girl completely missed the previous implication. Luckily, or perhaps unluckily, Healer Aguine brings her understanding in his next statement.

"We start praying that it's not lethal in the doses that have already been ingested."

No one says much of anything after that.

Things spiral quickly after that. The healers release Conner to his own room for the night, though Selina insists he be given a personal healer to attend to him through the night. Conwell, the older Snoweldon the dragon still doesn't know the name to, and Calvin all head to the great hall to meet with the city guard captains and to deal with stopping people from drinking the water. Selina hurries over to hug Cecily but stops upon sight of the dragon. Instead, the woman thins her lips and sends Cecily off to bed.

Cecily does try to argue; but being only eight, there's not much she can help with anyway. Now, alone in Cecily's bedroom, the little dragon watches Cecily sob tearfully into her pink pillows. She held together very well in the dining hall, but now the girl burrows into her bed like an earthworm.

He's not sure what to do. For the last hour or so, he'd just been panicking at the thought of being poisoned, sick, or dying again. But now, he feels as if he's gone a step past panicking and somehow ended up numb. He's still scared; it's just not very close to his thought processes right now. Or maybe he's in some sort of shock. Can dragons get shock?

Reborn as a Defective Drake: Snoweldon's Dragon

Cecily lets loose another loud sob. He twitches and dithers on what to do. Should he comfort her? He's never been very good at comforting people. If he doesn't, will she just cry herself out? Should he fetch her mother for her? Though, Selina really didn't seem to like him that much, and he wasn't sure the woman wouldn't just step on him if there were no witnesses. Probably a bad idea.

Cecily gives another tear-jerking sob. Well, he has to do something! No eight-year-old sorta-princess should cry like this! The little dragon looks around but sees nothing that can help him comfort her. It's just him. Taking a big breath, he pads over from his place at the opposite side of the bed. The doctor's prognosis had upset Cecily terribly when he'd first explained; Cecily had stiffened as though she'd touched a live wire. He isn't sure how she hadn't burst into tears in the dining hall. Hearing that one's brother might die is a heavy thing for an eight-year-old little girl to bear.

Somehow, the girl had held it together long enough to be shooed out of the dining hall and to bed. However, upon entering the room, she had set him upon one end of her bed and collapsed in tears at the other. Thankfully, she hadn't deposited him on a couch or the desk. Getting himself to the top of the bed to comfort her would prove a near insurmountable challenge, given his current height of a few inches. Luckily, he was deposited on the bed and can forgo that challenge. It only takes a few steps, and he's only a few inches from her blonde head.

"Cecily," He croons softly.

Leaning forward, he rubs his snout through her hair slowly. He applies just enough pressure to let her know that he's here for her and waits as the sobs begin to die down. It takes a minute.

"Little Sage?" She asks. Lifting her head, she peers at him with watery eyes. Giving another croon, the little lizard sidles up to her and rubs his head along her jaw like a tiny cat.

"Thank you, Little Sage." Cecily sniffs and scoops him up to cradle him against her face. She sits up and gives a few more sniffles while she wipes her face off. "I-I'm sorry you h-had to see that." She hiccups softly.

"No, it's okay. You needed to cry and let it all out," he warbles back.

He knows that she can't understand him, so he nuzzles into her chin again instead.

"You don't care, do you? That I'm a noble lady and I've broken my manners to cry?" Cecily asks tearily.

She pulls him away from her to look at him more clearly. Since this gives him a chance to examine her in return, he doesn't mind it. What he finds pleases him. The wobbly smile she sports and the sheepish tilt of her brow are much better than the sobbing she'd been doing earlier. Chirping, he rubs his head against her palm, doing his best to show care in one of the few ways this tiny dragon body can.

"It's so weird," Cecily mumbles as she reaches out with her other hand to pet him. "Yesterday was so exciting and good. I found you, and Dad said I could keep you and that you'd be my friend... and now...and now everything's so awful. Conner m-might die." Here, she lets out a little sob at the thought of losing her slightly older brother. "And a bunch of other people might die too, and--and we don't have any way to stop it." She sniffs and brings him back in for an emotional hug. "Oh, what am I going to do?" she asks the open air.

He wishes he could speak so badly. If he could only speak, he could tell Cecily that things would be okay and that she's only a child so she just needs to stay safe herself. Giving a sigh, he slides his eyes shut in slow resignation. The colorful flash of his second eyelid closing slightly before the first leaves him unsettled though. Were there more invisible dangers lurking beyond human sight? Thoroughly terrified, he sits up fully against Cecily's shoulder and uses his 'magic sight' to search the room. The floor lights with a soothing orange, and the ceiling glows with a tired white and gray design. The walls give him pause, however.

In tube-like structures, the poisonous green mana from the goblets and pitcher runs through various parts of Cecily's walls. For a moment, he feels mounting horror. There's a poisonous snake monster in the walls!

Reborn as a Defective Drake: Snoweldon's Dragon

Then, he actually thinks about it and realizes that it's just the pipes. Even with magic water sources, fortresses like this have to have pipes to transfer the water to where it's needed. Relief settles in his bones like a sugar crash. It's just the water flowing from the source into the pipes. Nothing to be alarmed about. No giant snakes to eat him.

Just as he settles back to trying to comfort Cecily through physical affection, some of his thought process catches his attention. He can see the poisoned water in the walls. He can see the secret water system that no one has access to in order to clean or fix.

He bolts upright.

"Little Sage?" his eight-year-old companion asks. "Is something wrong?"

He squeaks loudly. He can find the water source! He can fix the problem. The thought feels overwhelming, yet he knows he has to do it. So many people would be affected if the Snoweldon water remained tainted. The city could likely survive for a few days on alcohol or juice stores, but no city can last without water. They could dig new wells, but only if the water table is high enough, and on a mountain...that would be a miracle. There could be a stream or river nearby, but it'd be a logistical nightmare to transport enough water for the whole city from a distant water source. And, if they did, what kind of effect would that take on life downstream? They'd need a lot of water; how much water would be left for those downriver?

Reborn as a Defective Drake: Snoweldon's Dragon

No, the Snoweldon water source needed to be found and fixed. And he can do that because he can trace the magic back to its source. Turning to Cecily, he gives another loud chirp before hopping off her arm onto the bed. Like the previous evening, he makes a running jump for the desk. Luckily, he actually sticks the landing this time and doesn't have to scrabble to get up. Instead, he trots calmly over to her blank parchment and her writing utensils. Carefully, he wraps his forelegs around her quill. It's heavy, but he can lift it. But...it's not very easy to wield, and he needs to actually be legible.

He sets it back down.

"Are you trying to write something, Little Sage?" Cecily asks.

She scoots closer to the desk and watches attentively as he dips his tail into the inkwell. His control of his body has grown in leaps and bounds since he hatched. Hopefully, it will continue to grow, but for now, he's thankful to have the grace to do what he needs to do. It's a little messy, but he does manage to write out what he wants.

I can find the water source.

He looks up at Cecily expectantly but is confused when she just furrows her brow instead.

"Are you... trying to write something to tell me something?" She guesses tentatively. She runs a finger along the bottom of the still drying ink.

Reborn as a Defective Drake: Snoweldon's Dragon

He nods. Can't she see that?

"Um... I think you need to learn to read first. Or at least, I can't read your monster language. I'm sorry."

He blinks. He looks down at his perfectly legible English. Then, he looks towards her school books on her desk. A fluid, swirl-based script decorates the worn leather. Oh, right. He's in an entirely different world. It's likely very lucky he can understand the language here at all. In fact, why can he understand people here? It all sounds like English to him, yet they must not speak it, and they certainly don't write in it either. The first time he had tried to write something to Cecily, she had only commented on how he knew what ink was and how to use it. She hadn't commented on what he'd been trying to write, nor had she tried to allow him to communicate by writing like that afterward.

He shakes his head. Wait, there was a point in all of this. He's trying to tell Cecily he can help, not befuddle himself on the workings of the universe. He barks and darts over to the edge of the desk. To jump the full length would likely give him broken bones, but he can jump onto Cecily's chair just fine.

"Wait, Little Sage!" Cecily figures out his purpose only seconds too late.

He can feel the air displaced by her grasping fingers as he hops down to her chair.

"Stop, you'll fall and get hurt."

He huffs and jumps down to the floor with a grunt. His

Reborn as a Defective Drake: Snoweldon's Dragon

paws sting a little, and the strange urge to lick them comes to the forefront of his mind.

Ew, no!

Ignoring his body's strange instincts, he scampers off towards Cecily's partitioned bathing area.

"Hey, wait!" She shouts from behind him.

He can both hear and feel her footsteps as she races after him. To a creature as small as he is, the vibrations made from her steps practically sing to him. This awareness allows him to roll to the left when she grabs for him again.

"Hey!" Cecily whines when her fingers scrape on stone flooring.

Scrambling back to his feet, he darts around the dividing section. Luckily, the stool from his morning adventure is still there. Settling back on his haunches, he jumps to the first step.

"Hey, stop! You'll fall!" Cecily appears from around the corner of the divider.

Ignoring her, he wiggles his rear and jumps for the next step. Unfortunately, small hands wrap around him midway through and pull him back.

"Little Sage," Cecily scolds. "What are you doing? It's dangerous to jump around like that. You're so tiny, and Father told me to look after you."

She runs smooth fingers over his body and checks him for injuries. In return, the little dragon gives a whine of complaint and wiggles.

Reborn as a Defective Drake: Snoweldon's Dragon

"What were you even trying to do?" She asks. "You know the water's poisonous."

Finished with her checkup, she turns him around and looks into his eyes. He looks up at her searching blue eyes and gives a long huff. Squirming, he turns over, onto his stomach, and gets to his feet. Then, in the same hunting dog pose he'd used that morning at magic class, he points at the bathtub's water pipes.

"Something about the bathtub? Do you want to take a bath?" Cecily guesses.

She tilts her head cutely to the side. He shakes his head. Bending down, he sniffs ludicrously loud and then shifts about in his palm.

"You smell something?" He looks up at her. "Come on, Cecily! You understood me so well this morning!" he whines and rolls over, playing dead.

"You smell the poison in the water." Cecily guesses.

This time, she's more sure that her guess is right, and it comes out as a statement rather than a question. He yips in confirmation. Then, he wiggles and gives a whine while shooting the ground some rather hopeful looks. Cecily frowns.

"Okay, fine, but only if you don't jump on or off of anything. Father will be disappointed if I let you get hurt," She says as she lowers her hands.

He hops off her palms gracefully and immediately heads over to the water pipe. He scratches at the pipe and proceeds to lower his magic eyelid. The murky green magic of the poison guides him as he proceeds to pretend to sniff the floor and follow the poisonous trail towards the wall. There, he gives a loud bark, similar to a hunting dog that's caught its prey. Thankfully, Cecily understands this explanation much better than she had his previous attempts.

"You can track the poison in the water back to its source through the pipes!" The blonde child gasps.

The little dragon looks back at her with a smug, draconic smirk gracing his lips.

Yeah, that's what I've been trying to tell you.

He nods, as she can't understand his rumbling purr of "I told you so."

Hurrying forward, Cecily scoops him up and hugs him close.

"This means we can fix the water!" She announces happily. Giving a twirl, the girl swings him around excitedly. "We have to tell Father!" she exclaims.

Hurrying over to her bed, she plops him onto the pastel comforter before leaning down to fool with her shoes. The dragon peers down at her wooden clogs and wrinkles his nose.

Goodness, those must be painful.

He's almost glad to be stuck as a four-legged animal; at least he doesn't have to wear wooden shoes.

"We have to hurry! Maybe Father's not in his meeting yet." Cecily grabs him and hurries out the door.

Reborn as a Defective Drake: Snoweldon's Dragon

She opens it a crack and peeks out first. Satisfied, she shimmies through and carefully eases the wooden door shut.

"And just where are you going, young lady?" a stern voice asks from behind the pair.

Cecily squeaks and turns around in a stutter of clogs on flooring. Selina Snoweldon stands just down the hall from the two. Behind her, another set of double doors remains cracked; she must have just exited that room. Selina's eyes gleam in the dim light of the hall, but even her grace and fierce demeanor can't chase away the worry in her brow and the evidence of tears that linger in her puffy eyes. Though her blonde hair and clothes remain pristine, the woman can no more claim an untouched demeanor than Cecily could a few minutes ago.

"Hello, Mother," Cecily greets.

She dips awkwardly into a one-handed curtsy, the other occupied in holding the little dragon. "I'm going to speak to Father. The Little Sage can find the water source by tracking the poison in the water pipes."

He presses back against her stomach and away from the blonde woman. From the dirty looks at dinner, the little dragon knows Selina doesn't like him. He's not sure if it's just because he's technically a monster or if she dislikes him being close to her daughter, but the distaste and scorn are both certainly there.

"No, you're not. Cecily, your father doesn't have time for you to be playing around. This is serious; your brother is

Reborn as a Defective Drake: Snoweldon's Dragon

already very ill and you're messing around with that...that monster!"

Even knowing Selina doesn't like him, he finds himself surprised at the venom in the women's voice. Cecily, ever braver than he, continues on in the face of her mother's rage.

"I'm not playing, Mother. Little Sage really can--" Cecily's cut off by her mother walking forward.

The woman's heels make sharp clacks on the floor.

"Little Sage this, Little Sage that! Is that all you or your father can think of? Your brother might die, and you're still paying attention to some insipid lizard," Selina hisses as she comes to stand before her daughter.

Pale, manicured hands clench into fists at Selina's sides. To the alarm of the little dragon, they tremble slightly. Is she losing it? As in, having some kind of psychotic breakdown?

He leans into Cecily's stomach to be further away from the Snoweldon Lady. Cecily, unfortunately, doesn't seem to notice her mother's growing emotional instability.

"Mother, Little Sage can help!" Cecily objects. "He said-"

"Oh, 'he said'? Cecily, that's a monster lizard, barely sentient enough to know what's food and what's not. It can't talk!" Selina rages. "I don't know why your father insists on catering to your childish delusions like this."

Apparently at the end of her rope, the Lady of Snoweldon snatches the dragon from Cecily's arms. The feeling of her thin, cold fingers bites into his sides.

Reborn as a Defective Drake: Snoweldon's Dragon

"Hey!" he shrieks but quiets when the woman squeezes her thin fingers around his infant body.

He whines in pain as his lungs forcefully expel most of his breath.

"Mother, stop! You're hurting him!" Cecily shouts.

The girl steps forward to try to grab the dragon hatchling back, but Selina raises him high above the eight-year-

Reborn as a Defective Drake: Snoweldon's Dragon

old's head. He whines loudly at the treatment. Fear begins to cloud his mind as he isn't able to replenish the air in his lungs.

"I don't care. I've had enough of this foolishness. This creature is not a person, it can't help your brother, and it's dangerous to keep it so close to you, Cecily. Monsters are dangerous; they attack humans to harvest our mana. This obsession of yours has gone on long enough. I won't allow you to be hurt like your brother. Now, go back to your room. It's high time you were asleep for the night." Selina holds the dragon above her head in one tight fist while she uses the other to turn her daughter around and open the door to Cecily's bedroom.

"No, Mother!" Cecily shouts just before she's shoved into her room.

Selina slams the door shut with a resounding clang that echoes down the hallway. Cecily's fists hit the door loudly from the other side as Selina locks the room with a golden-colored, metal key.

"Stay in there, Cecily. I'll let you out in the morning," Selina promises coldly.

There's a crazed, searing light in her eyes as she turns her gaze to the little dragon trapped in her hand.

"No, Mother!" Cecily screams.

Her tone has taken on a frightened, horrified cry that sends ice through the little dragon's heart. Even from the other side of a thick, wooden door, Cecily's voice sounds eerie.

Reborn as a Defective Drake: Snoweldon's Dragon

"Let me out! Let me out!" The girl's voice cracks, as if she's on the verge of sobs.

The little dragon cranes his neck towards the door and wiggles as much as he can. He's squeezed tighter in retaliation.

"No, Cecily. This is for your own good. You'll see in time." Selina presses a hand against the wood paneling briefly before turning and walking down the corridor.

When she reaches the spiral staircase, she begins ascending them instead of descending. With a whine, the little dragon scratches weakly at the woman's hands. He doesn't want to draw blood or hurt her; he can only imagine her reaction if he did. But he does want out. It's hard to breathe like this.

Her grip is too tight! It restricts the airflow to his lungs and hurts his sides. Black dots dance across his vision like mad pixies, but he still struggles against Selina's grip. He needs to breathe!

Abruptly, he's shoved against a cold, metal surface. Selina's hand retreats and he hears a loud clang. Shiny silver and darkness fade in and out of his sight. Blinking, he clears his vision enough to see metal bars above his head. Turning his head, he's just in time to see Selina sweep from the circular room he'd been placed in. The sound of a heavy door closing echoes back. However, just because she left, it doesn't make him alone. Dozens of twittering voices rise up in her absence.

Small dragon!

Reborn as a Defective Drake: Snoweldon's Dragon

Dragon hatchling!

Smell good!

Eat!

Eat small one!

Jackknifing up, he stares in shock at the sight of miniature wyverns in a variety of blues. Unlike the wyverns he'd seen in the snowy valley, these beasts have interesting combinations of feathers and even some fur. Each wyvern is a little different from the next, as well. Some have only feathers or bright yellow chunks of fur on their backs, while others have no fur or feathers. Each wyvern occupies a small, rectangular bird cage with a single swinging perch.

These cages rest on a long, circular table that goes around the room. Tall windows take up most of the wall space above the tiny wyverns. From their clear surface, he can see the mountains nearby. Most likely, this is a tower room being used as an aviary for the miniature wyverns. He can see some thick leather gauntlets hanging on the center pillar and some cleaning tools. Beyond the miniature wyverns, the room appears to be empty.

He gets up and hurries over to the opening of the bird cage he;s been placed in. Not only is the opening a few inches above his head, but the latch is even higher. He rears up on his back legs anyway and paws at the door. It rattles a bit, but doesn't move. He moves back to the center of the cage when a larger reptile from the next cage over sticks a clawed limb through the bars.

Eat! Eat! Eat!

Small, wrong, preyyyy!

The little dragon shivers and hunches over himself protectively. The wyverns' calls echo around him like tribal war drums. Their calls are loud, in his face with their intensity, and scary in their intentions. The room's frigid temperature doesn't help, either. He hadn't noticed before, but most of the fortress had to have been heated in some way. That, or the temperature drops rapidly at night. Either way, he soon finds himself curling into a ball not only for comfort, but also to conserve heat.

Whatever temperature shield he'd had going through the snowy biome back when he'd been fleeing his home certainly isn't present now. He's not sure how he survived flying through the volcanic and then the icy region if he's shivering now. Maybe some magic from hatching? Like a layer of magic skin that flakes off over time after hatching?

He gives a long whine but can hardly hear it over the ruckus of the small wyverns.

How did I get here? he wonders idly.

Just a few days ago he'd been an impressive college student. Sure, he'd had a lot of work to do to pay for it, but it was good, honest work that gave him a sense of accomplishment. And classes had been interesting. Not necessarily fun, but at least challenging and sometimes exciting. Yet, here he is, stuck as a palm-sized lizard in a cold aviary with a bunch of carnivorous, monster lizard birds that want to eat him. He shuts his eyes. It's cold.

His breaths leave faint clouds of condensation above him. The stars and the moon gaze down at him from a clear sky. He shivers under their pale, loveless light.

It's cold.

He wants to go home, to his tiny student apartment. He wants to worry about grades and tests. He wants to avoid the flirtations of his neighbors and ignore the idiots who make fun of him for how he was raised.

It's cold.

He wishes for Cecily's warm hands or at least the softness of the pelts by her fireplace. He wishes for the warm sunlit stone of this afternoon, and the soft tones played in her dance lesson. His shivering begins to peter out. The wyvern calls grow dim and far away.

It's so cold.

There's something warm. It's strange that there's something warm there. It feels foriegn. New. Different. It curls around his cold limbs and lifts him up to cradle against something else that's warm.

He hears something. It's soft, but incessant. He wiggles when he feels something wet fall onto his back. For the most part, his body has retreated to numbness, so he only feels it because it feels so warm in comparison. Unfortunately, the warmth fades as the liquid drips down his tiny form. He wiggles at the discomforting sensation. Above him, the noise takes back up, sounding pleading but not as sharp. It's soothing. Very soothing. He gives a sigh and relaxes into the warmth. Maybe he'll just sleep like this? It's better than how he was sleeping before.

The numbness begins to retreat, and suddenly, the warmth is too much. He whines. The sound comes out thin and reedy, so quiet he can barely hear it. Something shushes him from above, and he finds it in himself to focus more when his body begins to shiver again. His head feels as if it's been stuffed with clouds, making him feel clunky and slow.

Reborn as a Defective Drake: Snoweldon's Dragon

"It's okay. It's okay, Little Sage. I'm here now," Someone murmurs close to his head.

Warm breath burns along his side, but it's preferable to the stinging his nerves erupt in as they wake.

He presses his head into something soft, trying to escape the sensation of his own warming body. The soft thing moves a bit as the person starts talking again.

"That's it, Little Sage. Wake up. Please, please wake up," she pleads.

He thinks it might be Cecily, but she sounds too scared and sad. She wants him to wake up. He blinks open his eyes slowly. It takes more effort than he remembers. What greets him isn't what he expects. Or was he expecting anything? He's not sure.

Cecily's holding him up to her neck and has curled her own body around his like some sort of shield. The dim light of the stars and the moon tells him he's still in the aviary. The thought distresses him, but he's not really sure why. He turns his head slightly to gaze out at the wyverns. They're huddling back, away from Cecily. Many of them strain against the farthest corners of their cages, terrified of the small eight-year-old. Not one of them makes a sound other than shifting fearfully or scratching at the bars of the cage. Oddly enough, there are bits of clear, sparkling ice on a few of the cages. The shards glitter prettily in the moonlight. The little dragon's fairly certain they weren't there before. Looking up, he can

Reborn as a Defective Drake: Snoweldon's Dragon

only see the underside of Cecily's jaw and the underside of her blonde hair. It's been braided sloppily into two long braids down her back, but some of it has escaped to frame her face.

He chirps a question: "Cecily?"

She shifts and pulls him away from her chin to look into his eyes. Relief flutters across her face, but he feels concern when he sees the state of her. Purple bruising pans from her left temple down to her cheek. Looking down, he can see that the splotchy skin continues all the way down her left side.

"Little Sage," Cecily breathes out. "You're okay." Crystalline tears slide down her cheeks. "Oh, thank goodness!" She brings him back into her neck in a quick hug.

He whines and nudges her gently until she pulls him back, away from her once more.

"Cecily, what happened?" He gives a low croon of worry.

Looking her over again, he can see that she's wearing ripped clothing, but it's not the clothes she'd been wearing that day. Instead, she's wearing a black vest over a white cuff-sleeved blouse. Her similarly black skirt, to his surprise, only goes to just below the knee. Compared to the other skirts he's seen her or other females wear in this world, it's shockingly short. White leggings cover the remaining length of the legs down to a pair of leather boots. He's even more surprised about these shoes as he had only seen her wear wooden clogs until now. He hadn't even realized she owned another pair of shoes.

Reborn as a Defective Drake: Snoweldon's Dragon

He whines and noses at a purpling bruise on her left hand. It isn't swelling, just bruising, so he doubts she broke anything, but it would have taken a good bit of force to cause such bruising across such a large portion of her body.

"Shh, it's okay," Cecily shushes him.

He shakes his head and noses her bruising again. He looks up into Cecily's blue eyes and gives a long, pointed growl. It's an immature, high-pitched growl, but it gets his point across.

"I'm okay. I had to climb out my window to get out of my room, and I fell," Cecily explains as she runs a warm finger down his spine.

She fell? From her third or fourth story window? He panics immediately and starts nudging at her hands. He gives several squeaky chirps and sniffs at her carefully. She bats him away with gentle fingers and gives a frustrated sigh.

"Don't worry, Little Sage, I broke my fall with some ice."

He gives her a flat look. Ice is not soft. He must be making an incredibly unimpressed look because Cecily grasps his intentions quickly.

"No, really." She smiles sheepishly. "I made a slide and slid down. I just didn't stop in time to avoid the tree."

She blushes when he continues looking at her blankly. She decided to slide down and ran into a tree.

That's not as bad as jumping from her window, but that's still...

Reborn as a Defective Drake: Snoweldon's Dragon

He frowns as he thinks about it. Honestly, he's kind of... shocked? At Cecily's behavior. She'd been so obedient to her parents and elders throughout the twenty-four-hour period he's known her. She's minded her manners, been prompt to each appointment in her day, and truly seemed to seek her parents' approval. Cecily has been the epitome of a well behaved child.

Though, she had tried to sneak an unidentified monster lizard into the castle last night. She'd also shoved him into the fountain when he hadn't wanted to be washed. And she's apparently taking self-defense lessons on the sly from her dance instructor. Probably without her mother knowing.

Perhaps he didn't really know her that well, after all? He nods to himself. Twenty-four hours really isn't long enough to get to know someone. Is it truly a surprise to find that the perfect child has hidden depths? What else will he discover about her? Is she secretly a fairy or a lost princess?

Unfortunately, Cecily doesn't give him time to think about it.

"Mother's completely lost it, Little Sage. I don't know what's gotten into her. She's never been like this before. That's why--that's why we've got to prove her wrong. If we can find the water source, she'll have to accept that you're not a dumb beast to be locked away," she murmurs. "I know it's probably not what we're supposed to be doing, but Father's in a meeting and Mother won't listen. So...so we'll just have to find it for

Reborn as a Defective Drake: Snoweldon's Dragon

them."

Cecily gains confidence as she speaks; growing more sure of herself. By the end of her vocal decision making, she sounds sure of herself.

She's quick to follow her words with action, though, as she hurries out of the aviary and down the long winding staircase. Awe rises in the little dragon's chest. Being stubborn or bullheaded is one thing, but this? He doesn't think he could have done it at age eight. He'd probably have broken down crying.

Jeez, what do they feed the kids here? Their hearts must be forged from titanium steel.

After a few flights of stairs, she presses a finger to her lips and shushes him. The little dragon settles onto his haunches and waits for her to reveal what they'll be doing next.

Peeking around the corner, Cecily waits a moment before stepping out into the hallway of the Snoweldon family wing. Now that it's gotten so late, or perhaps even early, only a few torches are left to illuminate the hall. For the most part, the stars and the moon provide a pale light that washes out the hall's normal warmth. One of the doors still holds light within it, and the flickering yellow hues dance under the door's lower portion. Despite the light, no sound can be heard from within the room. Here, in the thick of night, even the silence bound within the torches' crackles rings loudly to his ears. Above him, Cecily begins to whisper.

Reborn as a Defective Drake: Snoweldon's Dragon

"Can you track the poison, Little Sage?"

He blinks and nods his head. Right, they need to find the poison so that the fortress could purify it and have clean drinking water again. He closes his magic eyelid and looks around curiously. Down at Cecily's room, he can see her water pipe glowing as it runs under the wall and into the hallway. From there, it joins a center pipeline that has offshoots for each of the rooms on the hall. He turns to Cecily and nudges her backwards. The center pipe enters the hall from behind Cecily, likely from the center staircase. She nods and steps back from the hall.

The glowing pipe extends from the family hall to the center staircase, running under one of the stairs. Inside the central pillar for the staircase, a massive amount of glowing green poison sits inside what must be a huge water pipe. Looking up, he can see other branches of pipes for each floor and wing, each connecting to this central pipeline. He looks down and sees similar offshoots. Lit up with vile mana as it is, the pipe structure looks like a massive tree.

He butts his head against Cecily's palm and peers off the side of her hand in the direction the stairs go down in.

"Okay, down it is." Cecily walks quietly down the staircase.

Now that he's listening, he realizes this is why she decided to wear leather boots. Without her clogs, Cecily can move much more quietly.

Reborn as a Defective Drake: Snoweldon's Dragon

Unfortunately, the pair aren't able to follow the main staircase all the way down to the water source. Above the main hall, they come across light and voices. Cecily halts just beyond the reach of the light on the stairs. Should she turn the corner, she would be in full view of the main hall and the meeting occurring there.

"How are we supposed to just not use the water? What are we supposed to drink?" a thin, reedy voice asks.

Cecily peeks carefully around the curvature of the staircase.

"It's only for a few days. We're already looking into alternatives. For now, I just implore you for patience. This will pass," Conwell Snoweldon assures.

The little dragon climbs up her blouse to sit on her shoulder and peer around the corner with her. Below them, Conwell stands before his throne-like chair. Behind him, Selina stands with perfect posture. It's clear that she's there to provide the image of support. Several of the men he'd been seen with earlier that day stand beside him, including his aide. Some soldiers stand around the room, giving it a military feel. However, the gaggle of finely-dressed merchants and nobles in the center completely disregard that feeling.

"Oh, and what about those who've taken ill already? Will this pass for them as well? My son's feverish and won't wake up," A woman questions.

She's dressed in the typical Snoweldon region's attire of

a blouse, skirt, and vest. Like Cecily's, her clothes are not meant to be dirtied. The amount of embroidery and golden thread on her clothes could likely buy food for several weeks in some villages. Still, her visage gives no mockery or maliciousness, rather it only contains the grief of a mother. It mars her brow with sorrow and ruins what surely would have been an appealing face.

"We're looking for a cure right now, Lady Maldine. Our mages have discovered the poison in the water and have been toiling over it to create an antidote. We've only known about the poison for a short time; give us a few days, and I'm sure we'll have a cure," the eldest Snoweldon intercedes for his son.

Grandpa Snoweldon stands just behind Conwell, giving the impression of support and a united front. The little dragon blinks when he feels Cecily easing herself backwards. He looks up in time to see her expression sour. She frowns by thinning her lips similarly to her mother and pulling the corners of her lips just slightly down. It's kind of like both her parents are represented in that frown.

Cecily heads quietly back up the stairs and slips back into the family wing.

"I don't know what to do, Little Sage," she whispers to him. "The main staircase is the only way to get into the basement. Father says it gives soldiers an easier time of patrolling."

He tilts his head. There can't be only one way into the

basement. Not in a fortress like this. There would have to be air vents to provide air at least. With a castle this old, he's sure there are some secret passageways too. Unfortunately, the two of them don't really have time to go tromping around the castle. But, maybe there's a passageway that relies on magic? Or a clue written in magic? He's aware he's grasping at straws here, but this castle was built with magic; so, surely there's something he can do?

He closes his magic eyelids and peers around hopefully. The green, poison-laced water pipes glow ominously beneath the ancient floors, but he finds himself looking around curiously instead. Once he focuses, he can see silver characters scripted around each of the door frames to the bedrooms, but he doubts that's anything useful to him right now. He'd seen the same in the Annex of Magic. Most likely, seeing as it had been carved into the walls and portals, the script had some sort of enduring or protective purpose.

Looking elsewhere, he sees soft orange sigils drifting across the floor in a vaguely circular pattern. The sigil is the same as one of the ones he'd seen on Cecily's bath tub's handles. Was it the sigil for heat? Since the floors are heated by magic, it wouldn't be strange for their shared ideogram to be related to warmth or heat. Still, not what he needs, though. Casting his gaze towards the walls once more, he almost misses the silver-edged rectangle etched into the wall. It's so similar to the silver on the doors that he almost passes it by. Luckily, he

Reborn as a Defective Drake: Snoweldon's Dragon

always did well in pattern recognition and the smaller, four-by-four foot rectangle takes up significantly less space in his magic sight than the bedroom entryways.

He blinks back to normal sight and is rewarded with the sight of a wooden cabinet resting in the wall. It has a brass knob and is crafted of the same wood the rest of the doors in the hall are; it's just smaller. He looks back up at Cecily. Luckily his search hadn't taken too long; she still gazes at him expectantly. Giving himself a shake, he can't even find it in himself to feel embarrassment at this point when he takes the hunting dog stance to point at the tiny door.

"The laundry chute?" Cecily asks. For a moment, she appears confused. Then she brightens. "Of course! We can go down to the wash rooms in the laundry chute! There will be other stairwells once we've left the ground floor."

That said, she hurries over to the laundry shoot. Swinging open the door, she peers inside. Though not a steep drop, the shoot isn't a slow descent either. Neither Cecily nor the little dragon can see the bottom. He gulps. That's...a long way down. And he can't see all the way to the end. What if it turns into a severe drop out of sight?

"I always wanted to go down these, but Mother always caught me. She says it's dangerous. I think it's just unlady-like though," Cecily murmurs.

He's not sure if she's muttering to herself or to him, but the smile swiftly forming on her lips brings a shiver of

Reborn as a Defective Drake: Snoweldon's Dragon

foreboding to his spine. He's about to squeak when Cecily gives a nod, hikes up her skirt, and hops over the edge.

For a moment, his vision is split between the dark depths of the laundry chute and the moonlit corridor of the family wing. Then, Cecily tips forward, and he doesn't have time to think anymore as they both slip forward. For a moment, it feels like a playground slide or something. The feeling of his stomach slipping out of place feels about the same. The parallels only last for a moment though, as Cecily gives a choked shriek when the ground slips out from under her. He'd been right! The chute really did get steeper when it went out of sight!

Cecily fumbles in the air before she lands on the slippery metal siding. Her forward momentum jostles her into a wall. The little dragon is almost knocked from her shoulder by the force of it but just manages to hang on with his claws. Unfortunately, the rebounding force from hitting the first wall is enough to send Cecily into the other wall. This time, the little firebreather is knocked loose.

He shrieks and hits the cool metal with a hollow clang. Fortunately, he lands behind Cecily and is not run over by the speeding child. To his misfortune, he can't grasp any sort of edging in the chute and tumbles his way after her in a whirlwind of wings and paws.

Meanwhile, Cecily reaches out blindly to steady herself but continues to slide down the chute too quickly for her to

Reborn as a Defective Drake: Snoweldon's Dragon

steady herself. Instead, her hands catch uselessly against the sides, and her skirt blows up to reveal her bloomers. Luckily, the family wing is on the third or fourth floor. There's not much farther to go.

After five terrifying seconds of uncontrolled movements, the girl exits the metal tunnel and falls into a body of water with a splash. The dragon falls after her and finds himself floundering for a moment when he hits the water. Light reaches his eyes, and he's able to make out the sides of a large wooden washing tub. Then, Cecily rises from underneath him, and he finds himself sprawled against her soaked tresses. He blinks and feels the rapid drumming of his heart begin to slow.

Ah. They are alive. Cecily breathes. He breathes. They are alive.

He's suddenly very, very grateful the chute wasn't a straight drop. It could've been, and the two wouldn't have known until it was too late. Instead it was just very, very steep and dark.

He's drawn from his musings by the sound of whimpering from below him.

"Owww, Owwww," Cecily whines pitifully.

She sniffles and brings her hands up to rub at her tearful eyes. The little dragon sits up in alarm. Is Cecily hurt? She's a lot heavier than him. Could she have hit the sides of the chute harder, or landed wrong in the wash bucket?

Concern eats at him, so he wiggles his way off her head

Reborn as a Defective Drake: Snoweldon's Dragon

and into the water. He falls in with a splash but finds the movements to swim to the surface instinctual. He simply wiggles his scaly body from side to side and finds himself propelled through the water. Upon reaching the surface, he finds two cold hands scooping him up.

"Little Sage?" Cecily hiccups as she brings him to her chest.

She blinks away a few tears.

"Cecily," the little dragon croons and nuzzles her chin.

There is no blood to be seen, but only her head rises above the water. Cecily swallows audibly and runs a trembling finger down his spine.

"I'm okay. That was--was just scary," Cecily explains when he butts his head affectionately against her chin.

She sniffles a little and lifts him closer to her cheek for comfort. He relaxes minutely. It doesn't look like she's really hurt, just scared. What eight-year-old wouldn't be? He's surprised she even went to the aviary to get him. All of those miniature wyverns are scary! And she'd hit a tree too. It had looked like she had been crying for a while back then. Had she broken down and cried after hitting the tree too? But then, she had gotten back up and found him in the aviary. This little eight-year-old...she's really something special, isn't she?

He gives a comforting croon and nuzzles into her chin again. He can't comfort the girl with words for her human ears, so this is the only path left for him. He blinks when he feels her

Reborn as a Defective Drake: Snoweldon's Dragon

beginning to shiver under him.

Oh, the water's frigid, isn't it?

The coolness on his scales saps away his warmth, but Cecily's still sitting in it. And now, all of her fancy, layered, medieval clothes are soaked through. They should get out of the bucket and dry themselves off. Giving a chirp, he jumps back into the water to swim to the side. Hooking his claws into the wood, he clings to the side of the bucket and starts working his way up the side.

"Here, Little Sage." Cecily picks him up before standing and pulling herself out of the bucket.

A rush of water drips into the stone floor beneath her feet, but she pays it no mind. Instead, she sets him down and looks around.

"I've never been down here on drying days, but Mother mentioned it..." she mumbles to herself. The girl rubs her nose and sniffs a little but stops crying.

Finally spotting her quarry, she starts off towards the far end of the room. He follows her but looks around as he trots after her. The area they just came from is the farthest corner of the room from the entranceway. Eight large basins of water sit beneath laundry chutes that erupt out of the walls. Curiously, there are four laundry chutes with no matching basin beneath them. Two of the chutes have been boarded up while the remaining two seem to have been overrun with cobwebs and silky-stranded orb webs. On the other side of the room, work benches and tables have been set up. Several full baskets reveal clean clothes; neatly folded and ready to be distributed back to their owners.

Looking ahead, he spies the area Cecily leads him towards. This area has light colored, slatted wood paneling for a floor instead of the stone tiles the rest of the room has. Wires have been hung from one end of the room to the other here, and a few clothes have been strung up over the lines. He tilts his head.

Clearly, these are clothes lines for drying clothes, but how can clothes be dried down here in the same humid and cold room the washing is done in? Where would they get sunlight to help dry the clothes?

Cecily answers those questions when she kneels in the center and puts her hand through the slats on the floor. He hears a click when she retracts her hand. Something hums beneath him before a heated breeze wafts up from the floor. Looking down, he sees soft orange bubbles begin rising from within the slats. The bubbles float into the air before fading away.

Amazement bubbles up within him alongside a pleased croon. Oh, this feels like heaven! He lays himself down flat along the slats and spreads out his wings happily. The warm air chases away the chill that had begun to creep across his bones and numb his extremities. A few feet in front of him, Cecily flops down eagle-spread. The soft wafting of warm air can't lift her hair while it's wet, but he imagines it would if the hair were dry. He snorts to himself.

What a sight the two of them must make: bruised, scratched and sopping wet? He can't help the staticky, and perhaps a little hysterical, croon that rumbles out of his throat. Now that the two are sitting still, he finds his thoughts wandering. Wasn't this supposed to be a simple, easy way for him to help find the water source? It's swiftly turned into its own adventure. Still...this. It was something he actually might be able to do. He's tiny, but maybe... he could help with this? And Cecily is with him...so maybe he could actually make a difference here? Hope breathes fitfully within his chest while doubt wallows in his mind.

Normally, he'd never attempt something like this. Truly, if he'd known finding the water source would be so hard, he wouldn't have even tried. It's not like he's capable of much. He's no one important. Never has been, never will be. And now? When he's the size of a woodland mouse with no voice to speak with? What in the world can he contribute?

He sighs and presses his snout to the ground. Frustrated anxiety builds within him, but as usual, there's nothing he can really do about it. He has no voice in this life, but perhaps it was only mimicking all the use his old voice had when he was human. He couldn't do anything then with his humanity and his voice. What did he think he could do here with no voice and at such a size? All he's managed to do is get this eight-year-old

Reborn as a Defective Drake: Snoweldon's Dragon

hurt, wet, and crying. Why did he think he could do this? He's not anyone important enough to do anything!

He puts his paws over his face and shuts his eyes. This was such a bad idea. Why did he think he could do this? He's never been able to accomplish anything even remotely like this before. Darkness clawed at the edges of his awareness, and a sour taste stole across his palate. He sniffled. Oh, great. Now he's about to cry too. Let's just all have a meltdown in the laundry room today.

"Little Sage." Cecily's voice distracts his thought process from the darkness it had been going towards.

He blinks, opens his eyes, and moves his paws to see Cecily kneeling before him. Her clothes have dried. She's taken her hair from her braids to dry it, and now, the blonde curls have puffed up considerably with the heat. She gazes down at him with concern etched across her face.

"Little Sage, it's okay. There's no need to cry. I'm here, see?"

She comforts him and picks him up. The girl places him gently into her lap. He can't help arching his back when she trails her warmed fingers down his spine.

"You're kind of like a cat when I do this," she says softly. "But I guess, it's more like a kitten? Father says you're only a few weeks old. That makes you younger than me, so I have to take care of you. You're a baby."

He looks up at Cecily. He wants to deny her, to tell her

Reborn as a Defective Drake: Snoweldon's Dragon

that no, he was an adult. He should be the one looking after her. But all that comes out of the dragon's mouth is a high-pitched whine. As usual, he has no voice with which to speak and nothing truly worth saying anyway.

"No. Don't argue." Cecily understands some of the intent behind his utterance if not the words he would like to use. "We're both here. So we'll just have to take care of each other. When I cry, you comfort me. When you cry, don't ask me not to take care of you. Father gave you to me, to teach me and help me grow. I'm supposed to take care of you, but so far, you've been taking care of me. You helped me feel better when I was scared of my brother being sick and when I was scared after going down the laundry chute. You're really smart, Little Sage. But, that doesn't mean you need to do things on your own. One person can accomplish a lot, it's true. But two people can accomplish even more. Father said so."

He stares at her, surprised by her maturely-given olive branch. Because it is an olive branch. He can't mistake it as anything else.

Stay by my side, and I'll stay by yours.

Is it really that simple? Can two powerless people succeed where one powerless person would fail? Cecily doesn't wait for his answer. Instead, she continues with that spoiled child confidence he adores and loathes.

"Now, come on. We need to find the water source so it can get fixed."

Reborn as a Defective Drake: Snoweldon's Dragon

The washing room sits just off the main hall on the first basement floor. The water pipes continue downwards along the main spiral staircase's pillar. Luckily, with the water crisis, most of the guards that would normally be stationed down here at night are either sick or out in the city working. They only see two groups, and both man the treasury. It's relatively easy to avoid them by backtracking to a different staircase to descend past that floor. To the dragon's surprise and relief, the water pipes stop descending at the fifth basement level. Cecily, too, breathes a sigh of relief.

"I'm glad it stopped going down here. The next two floors are the dungeons. They're creepy even though we don't use them anymore. Our prisoners are all sent to the capital these days. It's part of the centralization effort of the kingdom," she murmurs.

The fifth basement level seems to have at one point served a greater purpose than the storage area it's being used as now. Like most of the stonework below ground, snowflake motifs line the trims, and the tops of the engaged pillars have icicle ornamentations instead of flowers or swirls. The engaged pillars rest halfway in the wall and sit ten feet apart. The little dragon doubts the basement needs them for support every ten feet, but he can admit it gives a nice look. Unlike most of the previous floors, the walls here also have designs and even some painted murals. The paintings are too faded for him to make out what they might have once been, but he's sure this hall must have been dedicated to something important once upon a time.

This area of the basement copies the above ground layout with a U-shaped hallway and a few rooms on each hall. Above each door, a different sigil rests. When he flicks into his magic-sight, some of the sigils glow brightly, some of them flicker dimly, and some possess no shine to them at all. Clearly, this floor had once been meant for something magically important. Unfortunately, Cecily's generation likely had no clue as to what it had once been meant for as old furniture, filing cabinets, and records seemed to have been shoved haphazardly down here. Peering down one hall, he even sees some broken wheels and a trolley piled high with cracked dishware.

Oddly enough, the stonework behind the main staircase boasts a light colored brick; indicating a different time of installment. Perhaps they had had some damage there at one point?

Regardless, he cajoles his thoughts back to the task at hand. The water pipes take a turn here instead of continuing downwards. They pass beneath the floor and past the wall on the other side of the hall. He assumes they continue in that direction, as after a few feet through the wall, their image blurs into non-existence.

He croons and points towards the opposing walls. Instead of a mural, this wall has an engraving in the shape of a snowflake. Oddly enough, the engraving has a 3D quality to it; it deepens at the center and becomes shallow on the snowflake's offshoots.

"The pipes lead here? But there's nothing here." Cecily steps forward as she speaks.

She runs a hand along the wall and frowns. He shrugs and chirps. This is where the pipes lead. Maybe there is a way to the water source in one of the other halls?

"This reminds me of something..." the girl mumbles as she continues tracing the imprint with her fingertips. "Oh! It reminds me of the toy Grandfather gave me when I made ice for the first time. He was so happy then. Dad can't make ice out of thin air, and none of my brothers can either, so he was glad that someone else in the family was like him. Everyone else has to have water first." She snaps her fingers in realization and grins. "He said it was a family heirloom to teach children how to control their powers. Maybe this works the same way!"

Backing up a few paces, Cecily surprises the little dragon when instead of taking out her wand, she merely holds her hands out and wiggles her fingers. Sparkling snow glitters its way into existence. He stares, entranced. Somehow, this feels different than when she worked with her wand just twelve hours ago. Instead of feeling neutral, Cecily's magic glimmers with the purity of freshly fallen snow. It feels as if he can reach out and touch the tallest, most snow-covered mountain peak.

An ice crystal forms slowly between her outstretched hands. He blinks at the sight. That should be considered breaking a physics law. Cecily's creation isn't pulling water from anywhere; it's just creating ice. He stares at it some more as Cecily carefully shapes it to match the engraved snowflake on the wall. That's definitely breaking an entire scientific codex worth of laws. Unlike normal ice, it possesses some sort of self-contained light source as it glows a fascinating bright blue.

Cecily fits her magic ice carving into the wall with a soft scraping noise. For a moment, nothing happens, and the dragon is left watching the wall in confusion. He's not really following Cecily's logic here. What does a toy have to do with this engraving?

Then, the ice sculpture sinks further into the engraving alongside the noise of winding gears. He rears back onto his hind legs as the wall splits evenly into four even triangles and slides away. A blue glow greets his flabbergasted face.

Blinking, he thinks back to his previous thoughts of not being able to find secret passageways in time. It seems the two of them did have enough time to find a secret passageway after

Reborn as a Defective Drake: Snoweldon's Dragon

all. He peers into it with amazement. Glowing ice forms a sculpted tunnel forward. The floor of the tunnel is paved with the same stone of the hallway, but it splits a few steps in to allow for a waterway to bubble along between the two walkways. This is where the water pipes end, it seems. Instead, the water flows merrily inside an open canal between the walkways. Vibrant sigils burn with enough magic to be seen by the naked eye from the edges of the waterway and from within the ice. Despite the ice, the dragon doesn't feel cold, and there's no sign of frost on the waterway. A bright light obscures the end of the tunnel from view.

"This ice...it was made by my ancestors. Only Snoweldon ice glows like this." Cecily lays a hand on the glowing ice with a smile.

She kneels beside the canal and reaches out for the water. Immediately, the glowing sigils heat to an angry red, and a crimson web scatters itself on the top of the canal. She draws her hand back quickly.

"Yikes!" Cecily yelps. "That's hot!"

"Cecily!" the little dragon cries in concern.

He wiggles his way down from her shoulder to peer at her hand. He sniffs it just to be sure, but Cecily's hand isn't burned, just a little red. He gives it a tentative lick and then recoils from himself.

Ugh! No! Bad dragon brain! No licking! You're not a dog.

"It's okay, Little Sage. I think I'm okay. I guess the magic sigils are there to protect the water. But...if they're here to protect the water, then how would poison get in it? And how would anything get in here, either? Only Snoweldon ice could have opened the doorway."

Cecily misinterprets his whining, but it does serve to get his mind off the...the...thing. That he had just done.

Thinking about it, Cecily's right. The zapping laser magic is definitely still intact and definitely here long before they got here. Furthermore, how would anyone get to the water source? Cecily's magic ice is the key to this door, so who else would have come through here?

Another thought strikes him.

Is this the only tunnel leading to the water source?

He swings his gaze towards the end of the tunnel where the canal leads from. He looks back to Cecily. This is getting dangerous. What if the person who poisoned the water is still here? They should leave and get Cecily's father or some guards or something.

Cecily doesn't pick up on his intent.

"The water source should be at the end of this canal. I bet we can find it if we just continue a little further. This tunnel leads out under the front courtyard, so it can't continue too much farther. It'll go straight off the mountain!" Cecily then scoops him into her arms and walks along the canal.

"Cecily, wait!" The little dragon whines. He squirms in her hold. "We shouldn't go this way! It could be dangerous!"

Reborn as a Defective Drake: Snoweldon's Dragon

"Little Sage, what's wrong? We're almost there. Once we find the water source, Mother won't be able to hurt you anymore!" Cecily looks down at him, but continues walking.

The end of the tunnel comes closer.

Growing more and more concerned, the little dragon nips at Cecily's fingers. He doesn't bite hard, but it's enough to scare the child, and she ends up forcefully dropping him. With a yelp, he hits the ground and rolls head over tail down the path. He squeezes his eyes shut until he feels himself stop, unable to take the dizzying blur of color.

Blinking his eyes open, he squints upward into bright light. Alarm urges his heart to pound. Forcing his eyes open, he looks around and realizes that he's too late. He's just rolled past the end of the tunnel, and he's definitely not safe. Cecily's footsteps echo behind him, and he hears her freeze in the mouth of the tunnel as she sees what he sees.

The water source should have been held in a beautiful central room. It still is, in a way. The canal bubbles from a central pool of water in the middle of the room. Deep within the pool, a vivid blue rune delivers water with glowing bubbles and sparkling flickers of ice. Several other canals stretch from the pool and exit the room through their own icy tunnels. Stone bridges reach over each canal to form a circle around the central pool. The walls hold inlaid planters where soft morning glory vines sprawl downwards. Above the room, a glowing, icy chandelier hangs from a vaulted ice ceiling. Originally, the

Reborn as a Defective Drake: Snoweldon's Dragon

room must have been overseen by gardeners to prevent it from becoming overgrown. Now, after being forgotten for so long, the room holds an abundance of wildly growing plants. An assortment of flowers--and possibly useful herbs--spread across the walkways and several of the more tiered walls. However, none of the room's natural beauty attracts Cecily's or the dragon's interest.

Instead, both children's eyes widen in shock at the sight of the figure standing at the edge of the pool. The figure only stands about four feet tall, but it radiates a sense of malice and unease that cannot be mistaken. Garbed in deep-sea blue, not much of the figure's body can be seen from under its heavy raincoat and large boots. It wears a strangely-shaped jester's hat on its head with green and gold tassels at the ends. Neither dragon nor girl can see its face due to the creature facing the water, but the dragon doubts he would want to. Despite the creature's relatively humanoid posture and human clothes, the scent of seaweed and blood wafts thick in the still air. This is no human.

Or, at least, not a living one.

Oblivious to the children, the creature stoops and reaches a hand down to the water. The little dragon leans back a little, expecting the water's protective magic system to activate in its defense. Right on cue, the system activates in all of its red, burning glory. Crimson lines race across the surface of the water. However, unlike the time Cecily tried to touch the water, this time the protection clearly has something wrong with it. Red and orange-colored sparks flicker to life along the pattern. Along one entire side of the discharge, the lasers shift to yellow and back again. More orange sparks flood into the air before that entire section of the protective magic goes out.

The creature chuckles darkly and pulls out a vial of fluid from its coat. Three yellow-scaled digits hold a glowing green bottle to the light. It turns the bottle slowly in the light, as though admiring its contents. Flicking the cap open, it pours a few drops of iridescent liquid into the pool.

"Funny, isn't it? How a simple bottle of monster blood can bring a whole city of mortals to their knees." The creature speaks through its nose with a crackling, hoarse, masculine voice.

The little dragon feels ice crawling up his veins when the creature turns to look their way. A single, malevolent yellow eye peers out from the darkness within the creature's hood.

"Honestly, forgetting where your own water system is? Forgetting the heart of your city? Forgetting the city itself? My, how the child does not resemble the parent. Or, who knows? Perhaps you do resemble that cold woman. She certainly didn't thaw enough to let anyone get to know her," the creature cackles and steps forward.

Where he steps, the flagstones darken and chip. A noxious cloud wafts from his mouth and causes the nearby greenery to wilt. His very form radiates a toxic poison.

"Not that I mind, of course. It makes all of this." The creature waves a gloved hand out at the room. "So much easier. Your stupidity also makes it easier, eh, Little Frost Girl? You're a lot smaller than your ancestor was, but you have the same look about you as she did. Just a blonde version."

He continues walking forward with even, measured steps. One hand puts away the vial of monster blood, while the other reaches inside his blue cloak to pull out a curved dagger. There's an insignia of some sort on the pommel, but neither dragon nor child take the time to make it out.

"I'm going to enjoy scattering your entrails before the feet of my king. He'll be delighted to have such a warm welcome after his millenia of sleep." The creature steps onto the peninsula where Cecily and the dragon stand and draws back the knife with clear relish.

At this point, the little Sage has had more than enough murderous cues. It's time he and his little lady left. He turns tail and runs to Cecily who still stands frozen at the mouth of the tunnel.

"Cecily! Now's not the time to act like a normal child your age!" he shrieks loudly as he slams against her legs.

The impact and his screeching is enough to jolt the child into action. Cecily lets out a fearful whimper, but within moments, frantic hands lift him against her tiny torso. He watches the world become a blur as Cecily pelts down the

Reborn as a Defective Drake: Snoweldon's Dragon

hallway.

About halfway down the hallway, she jolts to a stop. Blinking, the little dragon feels his own breath catch at the sight of an identical figure blocking their exit route. Only instead of a single yellow eye, three blue eyes burn from within the confines of this fearsome being's hood.

They're trapped.

Cecily's chest expands in a massive breath before she's moving again. This time, she sets her back to the wall and drops him softly to the ground just behind her. She pulls her wand from her own garments and brandishes it before her.

"Back off or I-I'll freeze you!" Cecily blusters to the two approaching figures.

White flakes drift down from her wand, a physical sign of her fear and lack of proper magic control.

"Awww, is the little frost girl scared? Trying to make some big noises to scare away the big, bad sea people?" The new figure speaks in a feminine, pinched voice. "Too bad. We've been waiting for this moment for millenia, and we know your family lost the skills to defeat us centuries ago. Those Ilvum maniacs may have been little immortality obsessed creeps, but at least they did one thing right."

The female monster withdraws the same blade as her male comrade from within the folds of her clothing. "They left you humans absolutely ripe for the pick'ns," She croons.

Meanwhile, Cecily stiffens and tightens her grip on her

own wand. Crackling fills the air, and the little dragon is just tall enough to see every drop of water from here to the pool freeze into hard, clear ice. As if a catalyst, the freeze spurs the two creatures into action. The female charges forward, covering the distance between herself and Cecily swiftly. Meanwhile, the male launches himself in the air and raises his arms in a powerful overswing.

"Run!" Cecily shouts before she bolts forward.

Thanks to her earlier ice magic, the canal is frozen solid. Cecily hops on the ice and runs up the canal, back to the main room. The little dragon darts afterwards, but he isn't half as fast as the female creature. The blue-robed fiend leaps in front of the Little Sage with an outstretched blade, missing Cecily's blonde hair by a bare inch. However, the female creature's strike has placed her just in front of the little dragon. With a great deal of satisfaction, the little lizard latches onto one of the creature's ankles by his teeth. Hard, almost scaly skin meets his tongue, but he only bites down harder. Ha! Teach them to underestimate him! He may be small but that doesn't mean he can't bite like heck!

The creature shrieks at an ungodly high pitch that rings around the ice chamber. He feels dizzy just listening to it. Then, he's forced to let go when the creature's male partner drives his knife into the ground next to the female's foot. He rolls away from her ankle moments before dark steel imbeds itself into the ice.

Reborn as a Defective Drake: Snoweldon's Dragon

"Sage!" Cecily shouts from a ways away.

She had run across and up the canal and had apparently turned to look back upon hearing the female creature's shrieking. A fierce glint enters her eyes before she's leveling her wand at the two poisoners.

"Get away from him, you monsters!"

Bright crystals of ice form in a circle around her wand tip. She jabs the wand forward to send the icy ammunition towards the poisonous creatures. Most go wide; they hit the wall behind the creatures, the floor, and even the ceiling with loud bangs that result in frigid flowers blooming and freezing in place wherever they land. Luckily, she manages to score two direct hits.

One hits the female on the right side of her head. She topples over with another earth shattering shriek as the ice flower blooms in a spray of foul, black blood. It seems that even her skull cannot stop Cecily's ice flowers from blooming. The other magic strike lands on the male creature's knee. It, too, expands into a flower with a spray of black gore. The little dragon squeaks as some unknown muscle or meat lands across his wings and spine. Disgust wells up within him as the stench of rotting, decaying meat floods his nostrils.

Horrified, he flinches and runs over to Cecily while shaking his body. Looking back, he feels the night's supper rising up his gullet at the sight of black blood splattered across his flanks and wings. The stench he carries with him does not

Reborn as a Defective Drake: Snoweldon's Dragon

make the sight any better. Before he can fret further, one of the creatures' cackling attracts his attention.

"Aww, how cute. What pretty, delicate ice flowers." The male leans down to clutch at the ice coating the remnants of his knee. The little dragon gags as the creature's grip cracks and breaks the ice to reveal the torn appendage beneath it. Without pause, the creature grabs the other half of his leg that had been blasted to the ground and reattaches it with a disturbing squelch. Dark matter slips and pools around the appendage before weaving into gory sutures.

When it moves, Cecily gives a whimper of disgust. The little dragon gags again. The female also rises from her slumped position. However, instead of breaking the ice flower that had bloomed across half her cranium, she merely spits a glob of black blood out and turns to their direction again. The blood hisses and bubbles where it lands on the iced canal.

"What are you?" Cecily asks. Disgust pulls her tone into frigid tones.

The creatures before her snicker, before drawing their blades once more.

"I don't think you'll need to worry about that much longer." The male grins at Cecily with malicious intent.

Even from his place near her feet, the little dragon can hear Cecily nervously swallow. Her wand arm shakes a little, but she bravely widens her stance. He likewise readies himself to run. He's not sure if he's ready to run towards them or away, but he's ready. Once more, the monstrous duo bolt forward.

The female sweeps her blade in a horizontal strike to emit a shot of green mana. Cecily throws herself to the ground in order to avoid the poisonous slash of raw mana.The little dragon is too small for it to have hit him, but he's not given much time to look at the dissolving, sizzling mess of where the strike did hit. Instead, the other creature has its sights set on Cecily where she's rolled into another frozen canal. He can't take the monster out, but he can slow the creature down to allow Cecily to regain her bearings.

Barreling forward, he sinks his infantile claws into the creature's ankle as it steps up onto the walkway between the canals. He pulls down on the rotten skin as much as can and is rewarded with a large chunk of it falling off in his claws. Unfortunately, it doesn't seem to have had much effect. The creature merely pauses to look down at him with disdain.

"Out of my way, pest," the male creature growls before kicking the baby dragon away.

The little reptile gives a squeak as he slams into the earth pavestones and rolls for a bit. His head hits something solid before he drops onto a cool patch of ice. Hurt blossoms across his sides but mostly where the creature's boot had hit him. That kick had been strong.

He blinks dazedly. The world spins haphazardly around him for a moment. He can hear someone shouting in the background.

Reborn as a Defective Drake: Snoweldon's Dragon

Is that...Cecily?

Concern brings him back to the present, and he focuses himself enough to roll onto his aching stomach and look around. He's sitting under the overhang on one of the sides of the canals on the ice Cecily had created. Somehow, the ice had stopped whatever magic lasers had been in place since Cecily and he had trampled right over the frozen canal earlier. Was that a design flaw? Or intentional? It would make sense for an ice magic family to do maintenance work on their castle water source by freezing it...

And, it really doesn't matter right now, the little dragon decides as he hears a familiar shriek of rage followed by crackling ice flowers.

"Don't touch my hair!" Cecily screams from somewhere else in the room.

Something makes a loud sound as it's forced into something else before shattering glass echoes in the chamber. The female creature laughs maniacally before being cut short. Thick gurgling and hacking noises follow. He's quite sure he doesn't want to see what Cecily just did. But, he's also quite sure that he can't leave a poor eight-year-old to battle evil corpse monsters on her own; no matter how terrifyingly capable she might be for an eight-year-old. He hoists himself up and hobbles out from under the overhang.

Somehow, he ends up a good deal closer to the center of the room than he had meant to. He emerges from the overhang

Reborn as a Defective Drake: Snoweldon's Dragon

to see a shockingly still liquid central pool a few inches from his claws. He had thought Cecily had frozen everything earlier. From here, he can see how some of the ivy planted around the pool had grown over and under the carefully crafted sigils on the siding. Some of the stone paneling had even fallen into the water below. He spots one of the fallen sigils gleaming up at him. It looks like the sigil for "hot" that had been on Cecily's bathtub. This damage is likely what's preventing the lasers from properly protecting the pool but not affecting the protective arrays on the canals.

At one point the plants had probably been well maintained to avoid ruining the protective magic. Unfortunately, when the ruling family had been subdued, they likely lost access to the water room, or perhaps had forgotten its existence due to weird succession. Either way, the water source had been compromised due to a lack of basic gardening.

A shaky tremor shakes the ground and startles him from his thoughts. Looking across the central pool, he's just in time to see Cecily dodge the powerful thrust of the male creature's knife. Spinning with all the grace of a dancer, she jabs her wand at his feet to freeze them solid. Unable to adjust, the creature topples with a wet, ripping noise as his ankles separate entirely from his shins. The male appears down for the count, only for the ice on his feet to begin sizzling and bubbling. Green-flecked tar foams up from the creature's feet and melts the ice. Within moments, the male creature has rejoined the fray.

It seems that not even Cecily's Snoweldon ice is enough to stop these creatures' vile poison. Everytime she freezes them, they either crack out of her ice or melt it altogether with their acidic blood. Yet, it doesn't stop her or slow her down. Cecily dances away and around the creatures as if she'd been born for battle. Ice flecks off her feet like falling speckles of light. Every strike of the creatures is met with a hailstorm of fierce sleet or empty air. Clearly, Cecily's 'dancing' lessons have paid off. She must have been learning to fight under her mother's nose for quite some time.

Yet, as skilled as Cecily is, there is no denying that she is merely eight. Even after only a moment or two of battle, her chest heaves and her hands tremble. She cannot keep fighting forever and lacks the power to finish the fight definitively.

The little dragon watches her fight with rising fear and dread. Cecily can't defeat these undead creatures. What undead creature fears a little cold or frost? Certainly not these. Though she might huff and force her frigid mana out of her wand in dazzling shows of light and ice, Cecily won't be able to win this fight. Left as she is, Cecily will die here.

Panic claws at the little dragon's heart for the umpteenth time that night. Yet, there's nothing he can do here. He holds no strength to aid Cecily. The male creature is impervious to pain, and while the female seems to be affected, pain alone isn't *effective*, just distracting. What can he do to

Reborn as a Defective Drake: Snoweldon's Dragon

help her? He could run and get help, but he has no voice, and with his size, it would take far too long! Could he even ascend the stairs without help?

The dragonet lets out a disheartened whine. What could he do? He doesn't have any way to help her! Frustration builds in his chest like leaden weight, bearing down with crushing fortitude. This was just like back home! Where he couldn't change things; and no matter what he did, he lacked the power to make people stop. He didn't have any power to do anything back then, and he certainly didn't have the power to stop things now.

The lead in his stomach bubbles as he squeezes his eyes shut. Shaking, he turns from the scene. *Why can't he ever do anything?* He casts his gaze about frantically. Ice pillars border the walls with other passageways leading out. One of those might lead him to someone who will help, but will they be able to come in time? Following the pillars upwards, he spies a glowing, chandelier-shaped object hanging overhead. Made of the same ice the rest of the room consists of, the light fixtures somehow glow brighter than the rest of the ice. Several pillars form a circle around the chandelier, mirroring the central pool of water below. However, not all of the pillars remain standing. The Little Sage blinks at the sight of several thick bushes and vines climbing up one of the half-collapse pillars and support beams.

Maybe he could climb to the top and do something?

Reborn as a Defective Drake: Snoweldon's Dragon

Bring the chandelier down on top of the creatures? Maybe if he timed it right, he could break the ice on one of the canals and activate the magic lasers? The fact that the creatures had avoided them pointed to the lasers having an effect on them. And some chance was certainly better than nothing. The dragonet feels no surety for his plan, but he knows he can't just sit and do nothing. The helpless rage churning his gut won't let him. Snarling, he hoists himself back up and out of the canal. He flinches at another screech of pain from the female creature, but doesn't look over his shoulder. Cecily has likely tossed another frost flower onto one of the monstrosities' joints again.

He scampers over to the fallen rubble woozily. Peering up, he feels himself sway for a second before he squeezes his eyes shut and forces himself to breathe. The pounding in his head does not abate, but he resolutely determines that this is the only possible thing for him to do and that he's not exactly big enough to climb up the castle stairs for help yet.

Releasing a sharp huff of air, he begins to claw his way up the dilapidated section of architecture. Being left so long without proper maintenance has left the stone with plenty of cracks and crevices to serve as footholds. He finds himself climbing up the rubble much more easily than he had expected, but he still clings to the cold surface when a particularly forceful crackling sounds from Cecily's direction. Shards of ice embed into the surface directly beneath him when Cecily gives an angry shriek.

Reborn as a Defective Drake: Snoweldon's Dragon

"Don't you dare!" she screams.

The dragon glances back to see her deliver a particularly frosty overhead strike to the male creature. Ice spreads across his head and upper body on contact. The being stumbles away only for the female to take his place. She strikes at Cecily with her blade, but doesn't even manage to catch a thread of Cecily's hair. Cecily dances around the monster's attacks as though she'd been born for battle.

Gulping, the little dragon turns back to his ascent and scrambles up the final few feet. His light body and strong claws finally prove their worth as he heaves himself over the top of the crumbling pillar.

For a moment, he looks down and thinks: *Wow.*

He doesn't want to fall from here. Then, another spray

Reborn as a Defective Drake: Snoweldon's Dragon

of icy barbs perforates the other side of the chamber, and he remembers the need for speed.

Shuddering, he pulls himself to his feet and scurries over to the center, to the overhead beams. Here, the ice chandelier is surrounded by a circular horizontal beam that rests atop the ice pillars like a crown. A chain supports the chandelier and stretched from the high ceiling down to the icy light fixture. Earlier, he had hoped to somehow shake the chandelier loose.

Now that he's up here, he can see that using the chandelier would be a viable option...for someone much bigger than he is.

The chain, like everything else, is made of ice. However, like the ice pillars and beams, it too has suffered the wear and tear of many years in this forgotten room. Though thick, it's obvious that the links are fragile. Even someone of Cecily's size could possibly damage them with some sort of sharp utensil. However, for the baby dragon, these links are almost as wide as his whole body. Though his claws are sharp and very adept at scouring footholds, they are not large enough to make much progress against the chain links. To cut through the ice, he needs to either become much larger very quickly or utilize a much more effective tool.

Luckily, he's pretty sure he has a tool capable of doing what he needs now. Heaving a deep breath, he sends his focus inwards towards the warmth that's been present within him

Reborn as a Defective Drake: Snoweldon's Dragon

every step of the way. When he flew through the different realms to escape the dragons and even on his ride through the city, the little dragon had felt a warm, curling flame within himself. At the time, it had felt like a natural part of himself, and he hadn't quite realized what it was. It was only when he had helped Cecily during her magic lesson that he had realized what that warmth was or that it wasn't normal to begin with. For while Cecily's magic feels like the softest fingers of frost dancing across his skin, the heat inside of him is a flickering flame spiraling in life-giving veins.

Like Cecily, he too holds magic within him. As a dragon, it probably should have been obvious to him from the get-go. Yet to his boring, human self the idea of magic still feels like a passing dream. Him? Magic? It sits ill-at-ease within his mind, yet he knows the warm tongues of meta-physical flames are not a delusion. It's his own magic, burrowed deep in his ribcage and nestled tightly under his rapidly beating heart. Threads of it trickle along his body in thin lines of liquid heat. It's small when compared to Cecily's frigid core of ice, but the heat he can feel from it dwarfs her frigid finger tips. What his magic lacks in quantity, he strongly suspects it will make up for in density.

Though he's not used it before, he suspects that he knows its most natural form. Carefully, like handling a piece of glass, he stokes the flames burning under his heart. They respond quickly with a flush of quick heat sweeping through

Reborn as a Defective Drake: Snoweldon's Dragon

his body. The ice under his feet steams with a hissing noise before he tamps down on the flames.

Shifting his paws, he grimaces as the chilly slush that squelches between his toes. Too much fire. Not enough direction. He needs to guide it, like how Cecily's magic had needed a little guidance to maintain a good form. But first...

He breathes heat back into his claws before taking a running jump at the chandelier. He doesn't allow himself the time to think about it. Between one moment and the next, he's momentarily airborne over the central pool. Below him, a white blur mirrors him in the crystalline waters. Then he hits the chandelier and sinks his claws into the ice with a loud hiss of melting ice. He squeezes his eyes shut against the vertigo as the light swings. The movement feels terrifying, and he knows looking down will freeze him in panic.

He can't afford non-action right now.

He forces his eyes open and breathes more heat into his claws to crawl to the top of the still rocking chandelier. From here, he can see Cecily's continued battle against the two monsters. She's been pushed back towards the central pool and is cornered between the open water behind her and the two monsters in front of her.

Perfect.

He pushes forward before rocking back to encourage the chandelier to swing back and forth. The divots he's melted into the chandelier provide strong footholds as he rocks the

Reborn as a Defective Drake: Snoweldon's Dragon

chandelier back and forth, farther and farther. It takes about five good swings before he's satisfied with the chandelier's trajectory. By that point Cecily had frozen the male creature's leg to the floor again and sent another ice flower at the female.

Fear quivers within him, but he burns it with the hot magma that is his magic. Now is not the time for doubt. It is not the time for fear. Worrying about whether he could do something, never helped him do it. Between one heart beat and the next, the Little Sage breathes out his fear and his anxiety and breathes in his devotion and care for Cecily. Determination grips his hot mana and curls it up his throat. Like a crown fire, the liquid power roars up to burn hungrily at the back of his mouth.

The chandelier rocks back and then forth once more.

He opens his mouth. And feels the whole world shatter. Bright white burns across his vision. The chain in front of him doesn't so much break as it dissolves with a hiss of hot steam. Bells ring in his ears and it's as if his other senses short circuit while his nerves and sight flicker. His fire shines in hot spurts of flame where it lands across the top of the chandelier. The dragonet has the time to blink at its dazzling brightness before he registers the fixture's descent.

Right. The part he hadn't let himself think about. This is going to hurt. The chandelier collides first with the female's head and then hits the male in his center of mass. The solid thump as it topples him is overtaken by the shriek he lets loose

Reborn as a Defective Drake: Snoweldon's Dragon

when he's knocked backwards. Both monsters hit the ice seconds before the chandelier does. Only, instead of landing on the ice, the chandelier bursts through it with its heavier weight. The ice cracks with the sound of a gunshot; and from his place near the top, the little dragon is in the perfect position to see the protective magic lasers surge to life once it does. Steam, dark blood, and ice vaporize in an instant upon contact with the piping hot magic rays. He squeezes his eyes shut against the heightened squeals of pain that come from the two monsters as they're hit by deadly beams of light. The chandelier beneath his paws grows warm as the lasers hit it too.

A bright light blooms across his closed eyelids. He's left with just a second to wonder what the beams have hit before the concussive force expels him from his place atop the chandelier. Which, good, because he was about to hit the lasers too, but bad because being flung away from anything at any speed hurts when one's this small.

The sound of thunder rolls over the room before the little dragon finds himself skidding backwards across the ice. The frigid temperatures of the floor do nothing to save his hide from the pain of rolling to a stop. Another boom echoes in the chamber before he's willing to open his eyes. The ice pillars swim into view alongside the last remnants of his own white fire. He blinks and tries to clear up his spotty vision. It helps a little.

Reborn as a Defective Drake: Snoweldon's Dragon

He's able to tell that the chandelier's last remnants have shattered thanks to the magic lasers hitting... whatever light source was inside it. Now pieces of the light fixture stick out of the walls like shrapnel from where the force of the explosion blew them. In accordance, his fire now also flickers from random ice shards and doesn't look as if it's going out anytime soon. Which, probably rates as a good thing seeing as the chamber's main light source, the chandelier, is no longer providing any light at all.

He blinks again. Huh. He's still alive. How about that? Exhaustion barrels into him in place of his previously hot flames. That... was a lot. He breathed fire. And crashed a chandelier on some monsters.

He has never done anything like that in the entirety of his existence. The ringing in his ears can attest to it. Everything feels strangely distant. Is he going into shock?

He lifts his head slightly to peek back over at the crash site. Beyond a few embedded pieces of shrapnel dotting the iceway, nothing remains of either the chandelier or the undead. He lowers his head. He's... really freaking tired now that they're safe. The warm ball of magic inside of him feels cool and dim while his paws and head feel especially heavy. The world around him warps at the edges when he blinks again.

Cecily appears above him, sweaty and breathing hard, but otherwise none the worse for the wear. She picks him up carefully and peers down at him with furrowed golden brows.

Reborn as a Defective Drake: Snoweldon's Dragon

Is she upset about something? He yawns and lets his eyes drift shut. The cold inside his magic has spread through the rest of his body now. Unlike normal though, he's not really concerned about being so cold. It's kind of peaceful, being so cold and quiet. If he wants, he can just let the rest of the world... drift away...

He... can't even hear his own... heartbeat.   His magic quiets down, solemn and almost nonexistent. He's never felt it become so small before. Sound fades from his consciousness. The warmth of Cecily's hands cools to his awareness. The beginnings of unease crawl into his mind too late.

This cold isn't a normal cold is it? He's used too much magic for his tiny, infantile body, and now it's failing him. He blinks his eyes open when something wet falls on him. Cecily's blurry head looks down at him, and another tear splashes across his ribcage. Well, at least Cecily is okay. He did that much, at least.

He lets his eyes slide shut. There's not much else he can do now. He tried his best. He thinks it works out okay.

"I am Cecilia Iceborn Snoweldon." His eyes open wide. He breathes in a gasping breath of ozone and mountain air.

"And I call upon my rite as a lady of the Snowy Weldwitts. I bear the heart of the mountain. Its ice is in my bones, snowmelt to my blood, and snow to my skin." Snow falls from above and gleams with arcane power. It twirls round to an unfelt breeze. A crown of light encircles Cecily's brow like

Reborn as a Defective Drake: Snoweldon's Dragon

a halo.

"I name you Frost." Like drinking liquid heaven, warmth pours back into his body. His cold core sparks back to life in his chest. His heart dares to beat again.

"After the first frosts that come in the fall to form protective barriers over the greenery, I name you Frost in the hope that you retain that goodness in all that you become. Remain kind, remain faithful, remain good, Frost." A new feeling arises within him. The light, the good, the unnamed emotion that's been growing in his chest take root within his magic. Change spirals into the flames of his heart. He doesn't fully know the difference, but he knows that after this he will never be the same again. An integral piece of him has been pulled and reshaped. Or, perhaps where he was empty, he now has something. Purpose- a nebulous, indefinable concept when applied to a sentient being. He has that now. It wraps around the core of his being and ties together the most central pieces of him. It's his name and it's his purpose all wrapped into one. It's *Frost*.

"You are a protector, Frost, and you belong to me and to these mountains. Be my dearest friend forevermore; Frost EverFire."

The ice underneath them lights up with a magic circle. The magic inside him bubbles over and tightens all in one instant. The fires held within his magic blaze brighter and hotter than he's ever felt before. His core forges itself anew in a

Reborn as a Defective Drake: Snoweldon's Dragon

blaze of greatness.

Heat traces its way between the newly named Frost and Cecily. Mystic cords, ties, and binds burn into existence between them as glowing strands of multi-colored light. One heart beats to the other with each beat brightening the spectral cords binding the two together.

"Cecily," Frost breathes out. *"You named me."*

"I know." Cecily whispers from above. "I had to. You're my responsibility. And my friend."

"Thank you."

"You're worth it, Frost."

Epilogue

The late afternoon sun beats heavily down on the duo. Spring still persists in cold mornings and frost found in the time before dawn, but the afternoon chases away spring's chill with the coming tidings of summer. Personally, Frost is just fine with that. Cecily's the one languishing from the heat. His dragon scales soak it up like a sponge.

"It's too hot~ I'm meltiiinnnggg." The noble child whines. "I wanna go back to the frozen chamber."

"You can't. It's under guard by your father's men. Even we wouldn't be allowed in and we're the ones who found it." Frost gives her a look through the side of his eyes. *"Honestly, it's probably worse that we're the ones who found it. Did you see your father's face when he came looking for the source of the explosion? I thought he was going to faint when he saw you covered in that dark blood."*

Cecily huffs and throws herself onto her back. She glares balefully up at the sun. *"It wasn't that bad. They never managed to even touch me. Absolutely no reason to ground us."* Her voice echoes into Frost's head, clear and crisp.

"He's your dad. Seeing you covered in anyone's *blood was*

probably enough to trigger his protective instincts. You sneaked out of your room at night, while the fortress was under high alert and came back covered in undead blood, telling tales of undead monsters poisoning the secret water main. I'm honestly surprised we're not locked up in your room for two weeks." Frost chuffs from his spot beside Cecily. He stretches out a little further across the heated stone in an attempt to pick up as much sunlight as possible. Sunlight, it seems, is one of the few ways he can absorb magic. Therefore he is dead set on absorbing as much as dragonly possible before any other crazy things happen. Plus, it feels good. The warm glow of sun-bathed mana slithers lazily through his veins before settling in his tiny core.

"But I want to explore the chamber! Like, where do the other tunnels lead? How did those monsters get in there? And what did the monster mean by forgetting the heart of the city? I need to knowwww, Frost." Cecily thinks over at him before shifting uncomfortably in the sun. *"And besides that, he didn't have to post guards on us."* Frost casts an eye towards the discrete shadows lingering at the edges of the garden.

"You wouldn't even be aware of them if not for me telling you." Frost rolls his eyes.

"Yes, well now I am and it's annoying."

"Just be grateful your dad doesn't know everything. Didn't you say it's treason to name monsters? I don't think even you'd *get away with that, Cecily."*

"... Yeah. I guess that's a really good thing. He'd have to

Reborn as a Defective Drake: Snoweldon's Dragon

exile us otherwise. Still, I can't wait to find out more about that secret chamber and what the monster meant."

"Back to this again?"

"I won't be satisfied until I know. I need to know. Something's calling me to know."

"Can't we just be satisfied with not being exiled and being able to talk to each other now?"

"Nope! There are secrets to uncover. I won't rest until I know."

"Technically, you're resting now."

"This doesn't count!"

"Doesn't it?"

"No!"

Eight more stories we'll have with you, have with you.

So-go- hang your hat on the weeping willow tree,

Eight more stories we have with you, have with you!

Reborn as a Defective Drake: Snoweldon's Dragon

Author's Note (Please read)

Hi!
Thank you so much for reading my book! It's my first time writing and publishing and I really appreciate your support.
Now- Please pay attention: What I'm about to say is very important.

I will be releasing FREE content online between books. These will be chapters that do contain important story information but did not make it into a book or do not fit into the book for whatever reason. If you want the full story, you're going to want to check out my website: www.isekaidragon.com
That's where you'll get access to all my free content, updates on how the next book is coming, and so much more!

There! Now that that's said, I'd like to direct a hugeeee thank you to my illustrator and twin: Savanah Townley. A big thank you also goes out to my editors: Grace Terry (my good friend) and Trudy Shadrick (my grandmother) for turning my ramblings into something worth reading. These are the people who listened to all my crazy ideas and helped me put them into order and a narrative worth reading. You can find out more about them (and their own works) on my website.

Thank you for reading my book. I hope you loved it. See you next time!
~Zoe Marie Townley

Extra Scenes or Cut Content

(The Un-Cut History Lesson from Chapter Eleven: To School We Go. This content was cut to improve the flow of the book, but does contain important lore for those who are interested.)

He mutters to himself as he does so, fly-away pages being lifted into the air with his actions. The little dragon raises an eyebrow at the man's disorganization and glances at Cecily. The little noble has closed her eyes and pinched her brows together in longsuffering. If he had to guess, he would say that Cecily is pondering the age-old question of "Dear Lord, why me?"

"Ahah!" Theodore cries as he finally pulls an aged and leathery looking map from in between a clay tablet and a pile of scrolls. "Here it is! I knew I put it in the Cramboyn period, just not where," he announces proudly as he relegates the books on his desk to the very corners.

Then, he unrolls the map and puts a book on each corner to hold it flat.

Meanwhile, the infant lizard finds himself looking over the map curiously. Instead of several continents like a map of Earth, this map appears to have only one large continent, though that may be because of a lack of exploration. The continent isn't just one large, circular landmass however. It's shaped like a very blocky or thickly written 'X' with thick island chains popping up at the ends of the continent's four peninsulas. Being used to Earth's very 'natural' looking continents tells the little dragon several things about this landmass.

The first is that it's not a natural landmass. Volcanoes and other land-forming earthly disruptions don't create cute letters like 'X'. This continent was formed by someone or something. It was crafted intentionally to be that specific shape.

The second thought he has, is that the landmass can't be very old, or if it is, it has to be maintained by whatever created it in the first place. After all, he's seen the Earth, and it can change dramatically in just hours when a volcano erupts. Such a pointedly-shaped land mass can't be very old.

"This is a map of Xevana, the world. Cecily, would you care to point out where we are?"

"We're in the Snoweldon province, within the country of Cavadeer." Cecily points to a purple shaded portion of the map that runs along the upper eastern coast of the 'X'. There's a brief, flat plain like area before the terrain ascends to mountainous territory. He supposes the Snoweldon province must be nestled into the mountains somewhere.

"Cavadeer's capital lies in the central plains area and is called Cavana. Cavadeer is ruled by the King and Queen but also has an advanced system of noble houses to delegate

Reborn as a Defective Drake: Snoweldon's Dragon

domains to." Cecily gestures to the center of the plains before moving her fingers eastward. "Our sister domains have several large port cities that we export minerals to. Hondarth is the northernmost, Cullmark the central, and Landrick the southernmost port. Snoweldon itself prospers off of our mining, exclusive trade contracts, and a number of rare medicinal herbs that only grow in cold climates." Now, she pulls her finger back towards the mountain. "Though we are primarily rural with small towns and villages in the valleys, we do have four major cities aside from Fort Snoweldon: Ice-a-too River, Longtun, Prima, and the South Blue."

The little Sage nods his head and considers it carefully. Being inland, without a trading port, likely is what keeps the Snoweldon domain rural. Even with some of the best gems or minerals in the world, being unable to trade them without high trading costs would definitely prevent expansive growth.

"The Cavadeer Empire's most affluent domains are the Ashlands, the Torrenbas, and the High Relkas. Neighboring the empire to the north is the Dwarven Free States, a collection of small dwarven city states that often partake in inter-city skirmishes. To the west lies the heart of Xevana, a land untread by mortals since it eats people." Here, Cecily pointed to the massive mountain range in the center of the map.

The center of the mountain range is empty though, lacking ink or details. Immediately, the little dragon lets out a confuzzled noise. Eats people? Continents aren't supposed to do that!

"Mrrrrrro?" He croons in question.

Cecily pauses and looks back at him before blinking in realization.

"Oh, right. You don't know," she says to herself. Growing focused once more, she begins to explain with a smile. "The center area here is what we call Xevana's heart because it's at the center of Xevana. It's also densely populated with powerful monsters, and the terrain itself is very dangerous. Something about the land's unique properties pull at the veil between our world and the monster realm, so they come through a lot in the Heart. The mountains shift around according to the weather, and once you get close enough to the heart, you'll trigger a mist that expands all the way to the borders." Cecily begins speaking quickly as she explains the center of the land mass. She clasps her hands together and smiles excitedly; blue eyes gleaming in delight. Like this, the child is a radiant display of innocent wonder and curiosity.

"Supposedly, if you wander too close while the mist is out, you can be lured in by the sounds of someone singing. When it clears, everything that was in the area is gone. Calvin said that the mountains themselves are alive and feed off of the blood of their victims!" Cecily says excitedly, in the way that only children who have never really been in a dangerous situation can.

Reborn as a Defective Drake: Snoweldon's Dragon

Meanwhile, the little dragon finds himself vehemently swearing off travel to Xevania's Heart. If he were to go there, he'd definitely die! He flattens his wings to his back and subtly scoots away from Cecily.

"Ahem," Theodore humphs and eyes his young pupil.

Though the corners of his lips bely his amusement, his expression remains stern with lowered brows and a wrinkled nose.

"Er, what I mean to say is that the Heart of Xevania is an uncharted land that presents dangers to many explorers and has not yet been subjected to modern forms of research," Cecily amends at her teacher's behest. She pouts childishly but otherwise makes no comment on the reprimand.

"Anyway, no one would dare cross the Heart to get to us, so we're pretty well defended here in Snoweldon, even if being near the heart causes the veil to be thin. It's why the King allots us a certain number of fresh graduates from the academy; we're the vanguard in the case of a monster attack. But, anyway, to our south lies the Duchy of Dartham. It's ruled by a duke and a council of elders, so technically, it's more like a lopsided oligarchy. West of the Dartham is where the wandering nomads live. Since the land there infringes on the Heart's territory, most people won't settle there and the Duchy doesn't want it. Instead, some wandering tribes live there, surviving despite the danger of the Heart." Cecily points to the innermost area of the western bay and gestures to some foothills near where the Heart's mountains begin rising from the land.

"Below the Duchy, the Allied Nations control the southeast peninsula. They're a collection of small countries that pool their weight together and vote amongst themselves. Some nations are technically city-states, but others comprise of several large cities. Each country has its own governing system and ruling power, but they all work in tandem to protect the whole when need be." Cecily points to the right 'leg' of the 'X' where there look to be over a hundred little different colored sections. "The Malacki Goben desert takes up the southern flatlands and is ruled by the Malackites, a tribal nation ruled by a family of chieftains. The South Western peninsula is ruled by the San Go Dynasty and works with thirty-five different heads voting on government decisions. That is what is defined as the modern human world."

The little Sage tilts his head in confusion. Cecily had only explained half of the map. What about the other side of the map?

"Very good, Lady Cecily. You've not forgotten our geography lessons," Theodore praises. "Now, obviously, these countries and powers were not always the way they are today. Many power struggles have shaped our world to be the way it is. Originally, it is believed that there was one united civilization across all of Xevana. Archaeological evidence supports this with similar motifs and ideograms found in the oldest of our ruins. We call this civilization the Origin People, as it is generally believed that all humans can trace their history back to it. Judging by the things they left behind, the Origin People had advanced magic, wealth, and good roads. Perhaps, they might have even had running water like what is seen here in the fort. It being a few thousand years ago, we probably won't ever know. We also don't know where the capital was, as we have not found it, but we believe that some sort of natural disaster occured due to evidence in some of the ruins that are assumed to come from that time period. After the disaster, the Origin Civilization crumbled and gave way to splinter groups that are termed the Tremor Civilizations. Most of these groups were formed from bits and pieces of society that survived the Origin's collapse."

"Obviously, with such a roughshod foundation, these splinter groups didn't last long, and the world fell into the chaos of small city-states with very little cooperation or economic structure. Eventually, this stabilized under the Ilvum Empire, a foriegn takeover by a species called Elves. These people were longlived and ruled over humanity for five hundred years. During their time, they committed what we call the Ilvum Purge and did their best to destroy all evidence of the Origin People, and all of the smaller civilizations that came afterwards, including a section of people we already talked about called the Corpheonus Groups. They also destroyed humanity's knowledge of magic, so when they lost control of

Reborn as a Defective Drake: Snoweldon's Dragon

the empire, humanity was forced to begin anew, without knowledge of advanced magic. At first, people couldn't do magic except by long incantation and very specific rituals. These had been left behind by the elves who themselves had no need for a foci to cast with."

"Humans, however, needed a foci for anything more taxing than basic magics and were left adrift after the fall of the Ilvum empire. Eventually, Focus gems were rediscovered in the South Eastern peninsula and spread from there. However, the rarity of the gems led to war until it was discovered that foci could also be crafted from the bodies of monsters due to their unique absorption properties. Now, I do believe that should have brought you up to speed with Cecily's lessons, if perhaps lacking in most of the details and contextual nuances of a more thorough retelling of time's passing," Theodore finishes with a satisfied nod.

Meanwhile, the little dragon found himself deep in thought and in awe. Elves had taken over the world? Cool! Well, not cool, as they seemed to have set on destroying all human culture, but it was definitely interesting.